THE COUPLE AT THE LAKE HOUSE

A Thriller

James Caine

Twisted Thriller Books

Copyright © 2024 James Caine

All rights reserved

The characters and events portrayed in this book are fictitious. Any similarity to real persons, living or dead, is coincidental and not intended by the author.

No part of this book may be reproduced, or stored in a retrieval system, or transmitted in any form or by any means, electronic, mechanical, photocopying, recording, or otherwise, without express written permission of the publisher.

This book is dedicated to my wife, who always believed in me.
This book is also dedicated to me.
For a change, I bet on myself when I made writing my career, and I'm proud of that.
I'm starting to believe in myself too.

DOWNLOAD MY FREE BOOK

If you would like to receive a FREE copy of my psychological thriller, 'The Affair', email me at jamescaineauthor@gmail.com

PROLOGUE

After speaking to the 911 operator, I hang up. I pace the kitchen back and forth, the weight of the call heavy on my mind. Adrenaline is rampaging through my body. I just want to run away from here. What if I'm not here when the authorities arrive?

In my daze, I realize the gun is still gripped tightly in my hand. I place it on the kitchen counter, and stare at it.

What have I done?

I take a deep breath and try to calm my thoughts. It's impossible given what happened.

I look around the beautifully decorated house and the scenic views of the lake from the large windows. Its beauty would touch anyone. I will be happy to never see such a view ever again.

I can't leave, though. That will only make things much worse. I must wait for the authorities to come. I feel stuck.

I told the emergency dispatcher everything. Well, most of it.

I wonder how the police will react when they arrive and discover what's happened. Will I feel the cold steel of their cuffs on my hands when they do?

I lower my head and try to calm myself. It doesn't work. My eyes widen and my face tightens as I see the bloodstains on my shirt.

"Sidney," a faint voice calls out to me. I raise my head, hoping I'm hearing things.

Please let me be delusional. Please let me be crazy. This can't be happening.

It was supposed to be a fun weekend. How could it ever have turned into this?

"Sidney," the voice says again. "Help me." Walking to the stairs, I look up and see the source of what's haunting me. "Please, Sidney."

CHAPTER 1

"We want to thank Sidney Meyers for her presentation today!" Vanessa Fleming yells to the crowd. The people watching me stand up from their chairs and clap. I'm bad at guessing, but I'd say there's nearly two hundred people in the room.

"Thanks," I say to Vanessa. She smiles at me. Vanessa knows it went well. We were both worried when I stood on stage that it would be a disaster. My behaviour over the past year would have made anyone worried. Vanessa is one of the main editors for my publisher, Twisted Thriller Books. She's also my main contact with my publisher. I never wanted to come to this event. I threatened not to, but my publisher then threatened to stop sending me my royalties.

I look back at the crowd who continue to clap. "Thank you all for coming today," I say.

On the large screen behind me is an image of my bestseller, *My Life as a Killer*. When I wrote it, it was more for fun. I never thought a publisher would pick it up. I was willing to self-publish it but was amazed when Twisted Thriller Books accepted my submission. A book where the main character is a serial killer, living in a regular neighborhood, amongst normal people, would not typically be a huge seller. People loved my idea of a psychologist who's an actual psychopath who murders and lies her way through everyday life.

Most authors will tell you that your main character needs to be likeable or relatable. Well, my book blows conventional wisdom out of the water.

My main character, Tracy Macher, is a killer. She's a terrible person who does terrible things. Yet readers loved to read about her. They were fascinated with her, wondered why she did the things she did. I think what many people wanted to read, though, was her eventual downfall. How would Tracy get caught?

In my story, she didn't.

My publisher tried to talk me out of the ending I wrote. They wanted Tracy to be discovered. For justice to prevail. I somehow won the argument, fully expecting the criticisms readers would have. But they loved it. I was surprised myself. I never expected it would bring me to where I am now, in front of a large group of fans at a huge writing convention in Toronto, Canada.

I never thought that anything I did in my life would lead to a room full of people clapping because of something I did. I smile and try my best to take in the moment.

When I agreed to be the keynote speaker at Readers Unite, I knew I'd struggle. My publisher reminded me of the obligations I had when I signed with them. When I showed resistance to holding up my end of the bargain, I received a letter from my publisher. The letter was full of fluffy legal terms but what they wanted was clear. Promote the book we published, or else.

My entire life changed when Twisted Thriller Books agreed to publish my book. I had written a few stories in the past, but none of them came even close to the amount of attention *My Life as a Killer* received.

I'm not sure why it's become so popular. When I asked my editor, Vanessa, how this could have happened, she couldn't answer. She did tell me one thing, though: write another one.

Easier said than done.

"And now," Vanessa continues, "we have a few minutes for questions from the crowd."

I smile. Oh gee, my favorite part. In my head I worry that I'll completely freeze if someone asks me a question that I didn't see coming. Thankfully, they never seem to.

This crowd is the same. How did I come up with the idea for *My Life as a Killer*? Which authors influenced my work? How did I start writing? They're all the same questions and I tend to give the same answers.

A man wearing a Hawaiian shirt stands up to the microphone the crew set up in the aisle. "Hey, Sidney, I'm such a fan," he says, his voice a little shaky. He's obviously nervous. If only he knew how nervous I am being the one he's talking to as well.

"Thank you," I say with a warm smile.

"I'm your biggest fan," he continues. My face drops when he says the line. I try to hide my fear at how he said it. I'm not sure why it triggered me the way it did. I take a deep breath and recover the grin I had before. "I even have a few of your books autographed," he says, the shakiness in his voice leaving him now that he feels more confident. "My question for you, though, is, I need more of you." Some of the crowd laughs. "I do," the man says. "When is your next book coming out?"

I smile. This is another common question. I have an answer ready for it, but no matter how many times I'm asked, it always makes me feel like complete garbage. "I'm working closely with my editor and publisher," I say.

"There's no set timeframe right now, but I hope it's sooner rather than later. Thank you so much for reading my stories and I'm so happy that you and everyone in this room is enjoying them."

He smiles as I answer. "Any hint about what it's about?" he asks.

I pull a pretend zipper across my mouth. "My editor will kill me if I say." The crowd laughs at my terrible joke.

Vanessa stands beside me. "That's all the time we have, folks," she says. "Sidney will be staying for a short while if anyone wants autographs." The crowd cheers for me again as I thank them all for coming. I stare at the man in the crowd who asked the question and he's clapping the hardest of everyone.

None of the answer I gave the shirt guy was true. I haven't been working with my editor at all. She would love it if I was though. They would love a sequel to *My Life as a Killer*. I just can't though.

I have a general idea of what to write about, and because my publisher wants to keep me, they agreed to the idea. What they really want is to talk me into writing the sequel.

The truth is I haven't written anything of substance in over a year. I try to give myself grace. Not everyone would even want to continue writing after what happened to me. I take in the crowd's smiles, cheers and claps and remind myself that I deserve my success.

If only they knew what happened. If only they knew how I wish I was never at this convention. Would they still clap for me?

CHAPTER 2

After the event is over, Vanessa rushes me over to a smaller room, where a table with piles of my books is waiting for me. Behind the table is a large banner with an image of me smiling, holding a copy of *My Life as a Killer*.

I'm smiling confidently in the photo. I remember how happy I was when my publisher sent a photographer to my home to take it. My world was spinning. I thought I could conquer the world back then. My book was already a best-selling hit. Sales have only increased since.

I had written a few books before, but with my newest release, I had become an overnight success. I had done interviews, podcasts, and contributed to written articles about my book.

My life changed entirely. Who was it that said money doesn't solve anything? It most certainly did... at first.

I was able to buy a new car within a few months. An upgrade from my beat-up Volkswagen that was on its last legs. Next, I paid off my debt, which was substantial at the time. I was over thirty and I still had debt from university from my Bachelor of English program and other terrible expenditures I had in my twenties. After eight months, I'd saved up a substantial downpayment for a new home.

My fiancé, Matt, was ecstatic! We could live in a beautiful house right away after we married. The problem was, when could we marry? Matt had a large extended family. He was used to big weddings and parties. I never cared for them myself. I'd rather have a small intimate group of friends and family at ours, but Matt was different. It was stereotypes in reverse. He wanted his dream wedding, and he wouldn't settle for less for our big day.

Sometimes I think everything about our relationship was in reverse. Matt was more romantic than me. He actually enjoyed cheesy romance movies and would make suggestions on what we should watch together. The man was a clean freak. He would be the one giving me crap about not putting the dishes in the sink or for not folding the pile of laundry in the closet that belonged to me.

Even though he made decent money as an accountant, I was the breadwinner now with my newfound success. He was happy about that, but looking back, I should have known better. Matt was never the type to tell me what he was thinking or feeling. He kept it all inside until one night when he'd just freak out on me for an accumulation of things I had forgotten to do.

When the publishers asked me to do book tours for *My Life as a Killer*, they understood that I wanted to limit myself at first, because the wedding was planned around the same time. Matt was the one who encouraged me to do the tour, and we would push back our wedding date. I told him our marriage was more important, but he explained that this was a once in a lifetime opportunity. I needed to see this through. How many authors would kill to be in my position right now?

We pushed back our wedding date and now it was to be determined. We still haven't set a date. I tried to get him to change his mind about having a large wedding.

Large weddings took time, and with the popularity of my book and my publisher on my back to write another one quickly, I didn't have it.

Then, everything happened to me, and life has been a disaster ever since.

I sit at the table and take a deep breath. I turn my head and the taller printed version of myself is mocking me with her smile.

Isn't this what I wanted?

Vanessa comes up and offers me a bottle of water. I thank her profusely as I open it and take a sip. Some of it spills on my blouse and I quickly wipe it away. I shouldn't have worn this material. The water stain is larger after I tried to clean it.

Great. Just what I need. I'm already anxious enough. Now people will know I don't know how to drink properly.

Vanessa asks if I'm ready and I nod. "Yes, you can let people in."

She walks over to the double doors and opens them. A small crowd of people with wide smiles on their faces start to approach me, and already I feel a sense of unease. I take another deep breath, wondering if the smile I initially had is gone entirely. I force one back on my face as the first person walks up to me with a copy of my book in her hand.

"I loved this book!" the young woman says. She brushes her hair over her shoulder and her smile widens. Thankfully it's an inviting one and my uneasiness fades a little.

"Thanks so much," I tell her. "What's your name?"

"Heather," she answers and hands me the book.

I take it from her and scribble my name in it, personalized with a small message for her. I've yet to perfect an author signature. I have a few signed copies from some of my favorite authors as well and they're so pretty compared to the monstrosity I just scrawled in her book. Despite that, she smiles and thanks me.

My first signature of the day and it went well. I was so reluctant to come here today and interact with fans, but after how that one went, I'm wondering why I've struggled.

Another woman comes up to me and again is very pleasant. She asks for a picture as well and I immediately stand up from the table and lean towards her. She takes a selfie and thanks me again. I sign her book before she leaves.

Second signing done. Even better than the first.

As I sign and make small talk with fans, I begin to let go of my tension and feel more natural. It just goes to show that things never play out as terribly as you think they will. I'm not sure what I thought would happen today, but so far, everything has gone swimmingly.

A teenage girl thanks me after I sign her copy. She has such a beautiful smile and the aura around her is pure happiness to be near me. It truly melts my heart knowing that she's this way because of something I created. She tells me she's a writer herself and hopes to be like me some day.

I love knowing that I've inspired a young reader and writer like her.

Next is someone I recognize from the event. The man with the Hawaiian shirt. He smiles at me as I give a thin one back myself.

"I know I said this before," he says, "but I really

am your biggest fan." I take a deep breath when he says those words again. It irked me at the event when he did, and I tried to play it off. It's harder to do now when he's standing in front of me and repeating it. "Are you okay?" he asks.

I catch myself in my thoughts and give a wide smile. "Sorry, I must admit I'm very tired. Long day. Thank you for your question at the event, and for reading my book." He hands me a book to sign and I sigh when I look at the cover depicting the back of a young girl on a swing at night. "*The Girl I Knew*," I say. "I didn't even know you could buy a copy of this book anymore."

"They don't sell it anymore at stores or online," the man confirms. "I had to scour the net to find a copy. After I read *My Life as a Killer*, I had to buy everything you wrote. That book was my favourite, though. It was such a page-turning thriller. I've never read anything like it. A whole book from the antagonist's viewpoint. It was astounding. I never thought I'd feel so much empathy for a terrible character."

I smile, this time genuinely. "Thanks. It was something I always wanted to write. It wasn't picked up by a publisher for a long time, and for obvious reasons."

He laughs. "Not exactly your typical main character. I loved it!"

I ask for his name and sign the book, taking a moment to look at my cover. It was the first book I wrote. I remember thinking it would move worlds for me after it was published. It made a few dollars, but it was nothing like what I thought a published author would make.

Then I wrote *My Life as a Killer* and made much more than I thought I ever could from writing.

I hand the book to the man, who's ecstatic. "Anyway,

can I get a picture?" he asks, taking out his cell.

I nod. "For my number one fan, anything." I stand up from the table and he leans back beside me as he aims the camera. Before taking the picture, he wraps his arm around my shoulder. I try to hide the sensation of fear, worrying he caught my expression in the photo.

I'd prefer he didn't touch me. I'd prefer not to be here entirely. My hand begins to tremble. I grab it and hold it tightly, taking a deep breath, and try to manage my emotions.

He thanks me profusely as he leaves. I watch him as he does, and for a moment, he looks back at me, his smile growing wider before leaving through the double doors.

I wonder, is the Hawaiian shirt guy the one who ruined my life? Will I ever discover who it was?

I take a deep breath before signing the next book.

CHAPTER 3

I thank the people running the show before I leave. The hotel I'm staying at is connected to the hall and it's only a few minutes before I'll be back in my room. I sigh with relief knowing this day is over.

I've never been an extroverted person. The idea of doing what I did today is exhausting. After my presentation and book signing, all I want to do is take a nap and hibernate in my room. No doubt Matt will be out. Since coming to Toronto, he's been such a tourist. He's been travelling around all week, taking in the sights and the many things the city has to offer.

We don't do much in Chestermere. I'm a homebody by nature. He's the opposite. He's always trying to get me to go places, and usually I reluctantly agree to come with him.

I was so happy when Matt took time off from work to come to the convention with me. He knew how nervous I was. I assumed that meant he would be there to support me today for my event.

I was upset when he wasn't there. He knew how anxious I was about doing it. He knew how concerned I was about the signing. About being around fans. I was hoping he would be nearby, just to at least have his presence there. Help make me feel a little more comfortable.

I wonder what could have been more important.

As I enter the hotel lobby, a woman in her twenties smiles at me. It's an expression I'm getting used to since arriving at the convention. Recognition.

"Oh my god!" she shouts. "You're Sidney Meyers. Can I have an autograph?" She takes a step towards me. "I'm your biggest fan."

I'm not sure what it is about her. The enthusiasm in her face seems genuine enough. She seems innocent and harmless as well. But I immediately flinch as she gets closer to me. Without saying a word, I scurry past her and head towards the elevator. I press the button, but no doors open for me. I breathe in deep and look back at the young fan, who's staring at me.

She's probably thinking the same thing I am. What's wrong with you? I take another deep breath and, too impatient for the elevator to arrive, instead take the stairs. I'm only on the fourth floor. If it wasn't for my heels, it wouldn't be difficult at all to climb.

My shoes echo in the empty stairwell. I try to calm myself, wondering why I freaked out that way. She was probably just another fan, yet I reacted like she was a maniac.

This was what I feared I would be like today. I was worried I'd clam up like a scared turtle and implode on stage. When that didn't happen, I literally thought I'd explode at the book signing.

I was scared the entire time being around people. I thought maybe I would just walk off at the slightest fear. Ditch the event. Readers would see the real me.

I used to love interacting with fans. My book was a hit right from the weekend it was published. I knew my life would change; I just never thought it would be for the worse.

At the beginning, I would reply to every fan's email or post about me on Facebook. I was so thankful that they loved my writing to the point that they wanted to reach out to me.

As I get to the second floor, the stairwell door on the first floor opens and slams closed. I hear footsteps coming up. My breathing quickens as I hurry up the stairs.

I used to love interacting with fans. I used to love being a writer. The truth is, I haven't written a word in a very long time. I knew that notoriety came with its downfalls. I never suspected it would impact me like this.

The footsteps coming up the stairs start to quicken as well, and my heart beats faster. As much as my heels will allow, I run to the third-floor door and open it. I don't care that my room is on the fourth. I can't be in this stairwell.

When I'm on the third floor, I close the door behind me and don't look back as I hurry down the hallway. I have no clue where I'm going.

Suddenly I hear the stairwell door open and a man in a suit comes out, walking down the opposite hallway from me. I take another deep breath and lower my head.

I never used to be like this. Scared. I'm not even sure what I'm afraid of.

Everything changed when I received that first of many emails from one reader. The header read, "I'm your biggest fan". I clicked on the email from someone named IWriteAlone2009. It was from a Gmail account. The fan went into how much they loved *My Life as a Killer*. They went over some of their favorite scenes of the book, which for them was the graphic ways people were murdered. It put me off. It wasn't the first email like this

I'd received, though. The writer of the email never named themselves anything other than IWriteAlone2009. At the bottom of the email, they wrote: "From your number one fan."

I wondered who they were. I imagined a creative young woman who must feel very lonely. Writing can be a very isolating occupation. You're not typically around people. Was 2009 an indication of how old they were or just random numbers?

I replied back how I usually do, thanking them for reading and saying how happy I was that they liked my story. Soon after, though, I received another email from my number one fan.

It started innocently enough. IWriteAlone told me how much they enjoyed some of my other books as well. They let me know how they would buy all the rest of my books and anything I wrote in the future. A few days later, they emailed me again with praise of how they enjoyed some of my older books.

Then it started to get more personal, which I was okay with. IWriteAlone started asking me questions about my writing process and how I get into the mindset to think of the ideas I have. I answered them all, and promptly as well. I loved answering questions like this from fans. IWriteAlone said they wanted to become a writer like me, and I loved the idea that maybe I could inspire them to take a chance on their creativity.

It didn't go that way.

First, the aura of the emails changed. IWriteAlone started expressing more and more self-loathing at how they were not a published author, and I was. They put themselves down continuously and made fun of their inability to write a story. IWriteAlone said they weren't good enough to be like me.

I tried to reassure her that it was okay to feel this way. I say *her*, even though they never shared their name, gender or anything personal about themselves. I assumed it was a young woman based on what she wrote, but I never confirmed it.

One of the emails from IWriteAlone said she would "kill" to be like me, and that I should be "thankful every day" that I wasn't like her. This time I didn't reply back. There was something ominous about the email. Context matters. Perhaps she hadn't meant to come off the way she had. It's hard to tell when it's in an email.

To me, what she wrote was concerning at the least. If she was a friend, I'd have gone to her house to check on her. I didn't know anything about IWriteAlone, though, my number one fan.

I thought about asking her for more personal details. Where did she live? What was her first name? Something that I could use to confirm more about who she might be. By this time, I had already received well over thirty emails within a few weeks. I was concerned. I worried that the self loathing and hatred she seemed to have for herself could turn into self-harm.

I didn't reply to her email, though.

I was going on a trip with Matt for the week. We wanted to celebrate the success of *My Life as a Killer* by going to this resort in the Rocky Mountains. Matt made me promise him to not take my phone or laptop with me on the trip. I had to, though. I had tasks I needed to complete, even if I was on vacation.

He was getting more and more upset about me and how much time I was spending on my work as an author. I knew even back then that he was somewhat resentful of me pushing back the wedding, but as he told me, this was a once in a lifetime opportunity. I had to make the best of it I could.

When we came back from our vacation, I had many emails waiting for my reply. Emails that still make me cringe when I think of them today. Some were from my publisher and fans; I had a few regulars who would email me frequently. I enjoyed speaking with fans. I didn't have coworkers anymore. It was as if these readers had become them.

Those didn't bother me. I usually looked forward to replying to them. What did were the multiple emails from IWriteAlone. How many emails can one person send in a week? The answer: forty-one. I counted.

The oldest was harmless enough. "Hey," IWriteAlone wrote, "I just finished another of your books! Now I've read them all! You need to write more so I have something to do. Sincerely, your number one fan."

The next was written with a much different tone. "Why haven't you replied to me!" the email header read. When I clicked on it, IWriteAlone said how they took the time to write to me and was upset when I didn't reply.

I should have put on an out of office reply so that anyone who wrote while I was away would have received an email that I was gone until a certain date. I sometimes wonder what would have happened if I did. Could I have avoided everything that came after?

The email that followed was written in all capital letters. "I HATE YOU!" The email had several swearwords sprinkled in. The self-loathing she had for herself was beginning to turn to anger and rage towards me.

The emails after seemed to all have the same tone, each in all capitals. "YOU SHOULD TREAT YOUR FANS

BETTER THAN THIS!" "I DON'T DESERVE THIS!" "I WISH YOU NOTHING BUT THE WORST!"

I read every single one of her emails. I didn't even bother opening the ones from other people. I was so focused on how someone who claimed to be my number one fan could turn so quickly against me.

With each email, I felt my heart beat faster. I felt out of breath reading her harsh words towards me. If someone had said all this to my face, I'd be terrified. Even though they were virtual sentences, they still had the same impact. I was afraid. Who was IWriteAlone2009?

There was something maddening about this person. I was scared at the idea of ever meeting someone like them. She could literally be anyone. I had no clue what she looked like.

When I got to her final message, I held my breath. This time there were no all-capital sentences. The email header read: "You're finished." I opened the email, reminding myself to breathe before I passed out. "You will get what you deserve." That was it. That was all she wrote.

I still remember how frightened I was as I read that last message. If the words she wrote weren't scary enough, beneath the text was a picture. I recognized the location immediately. It was a café near where I lived. I enjoyed writing there sometimes. I'd always sit in the same location if I could. The café's large windows faced the street, and I enjoyed watching the activity outside as I wrote.

As I examined the picture, my mouth dropped. I could see myself sitting at the table in the cafe, looking out the windows.

I catch my breath in the hallway on the third floor

of the hotel, remembering what happened to me. I look down the empty hallway. When I'm confident that the man who was behind me is gone, I work up the courage to go back to the stairwell door. I take a deep breath as I open it. When I step into the stairwell, it's quiet. Too quiet. It's so echoey that you could hear a pin drop. It's only a few steps to get to the fourth floor, but I can't get myself to take a single one. My hand is trembling out of control.

I close the door and go back into the third floor, striking the elevator button hard. I slow my breathing, checking my pulse with my finger. I can feel it slow down with my longer breaths.

That wasn't the last email that IWriteAlone sent me. Soon, there were more pictures. These ones had no text, just photos. One of them was me in the street walking to my car. Another was of my apartment building.

I called the police, but they didn't do anything about it. IWriteAlone committed no crimes, they told me.

Out of anxiety, I stopped reading my emails entirely. Matt was concerned about how I was doing and encouraged me to delete my entire account. I was scared though. I couldn't. I needed to see what IWriteAlone was going to send next. It was a way to know where they were or who they could be.

I didn't delete my account, but Matt talked me into signing out and not logging back in.

Now no one could get a hold of me. No fans, nor my editor, Vanessa. Not even my publisher. I wanted nothing to do with anybody.

I barely left my house, and when I did, Matt was beside me. I couldn't bear the thought that someone could be out there, watching me. Taking pictures. IWriteAlone could walk past me, and I wouldn't know.

Despite all the money I made from writing, I'd give it all back. It isn't worth what happened to me. I'm scared of everything.

All I ever wanted to do was write a book. Ever since I was a teenager and fell in love with reading. Then I did. Soon I wrote another, and another. Then I wrote *My Life as a Killer*. It changed everything, and not for the better.

My writing came to an abrupt stop after IWriteAlone. I couldn't write a complete sentence after. I'd only speak with my publisher on the phone. At first, they encouraged me to keep writing. Write one sentence. One word on a page. One foot in front of the other.

I couldn't.

They offered to pay for trauma therapy.

I refused. It was easier to not think about IWriteAlone.

I wish I could go back in time and never be a writer.

My publisher was becoming more and more upset with my reluctance to do anything. They threatened to stop paying my royalties if I didn't fulfill what I promised them when I inked the deal they gave me. *My Life as a Killer* was still a major success, and I wanted my checks to continue. I had to put in some work, including this convention and the book signing today.

There will be more to come, though.

The elevator door opens, and I step inside. An older couple with welcoming smiles greets me. I give a thin smile and hit the fourth-floor button. The woman raises an eyebrow to her husband when she sees me going up one floor. I can only imagine what the pair are thinking.

When I exit the elevator onto my floor, I head toward my room, taking my passkey out. How could my life change so quickly? After *My Life as a Killer* was released, I felt on top of the world... until IWriteAlone entered my life.

Now I can't write. My life as an author is about to implode.

I wish I could say things with Matt have improved. I thought he was going to be happy once I wasn't writing and could spend more time with him.

That wasn't the case either.

My relationship with Matt is all I have left and even that is on the edge after what he did. Sometimes I wonder why I'm still with him. How can I still be engaged to him now my trust in him is broken beyond repair?

I approach my room and stand outside, staring at the door. I take another deep breath and I'm about to swipe my pass to unlock the door when I realize it's slightly open. This is the third time since we arrived at the hotel that the door hasn't fully closed. I told Matt about it and thought we should get a new room, but he wasn't worried.

I push the door open and enter the room. Matt is on the bed, watching television. He smiles at me as I walk in. I force myself to smile back.

I wish I was anyone but me.

CHAPTER 4

"Hey," Matt says, his grin widening. "So, how was it?" He turns off the television and waits for me to respond.

I flick my leg and my high heel flies off my foot. I toss the second and plop myself on the bed beside him.

I wonder if Matt missed my event and book signing because of something he was watching. I try to not get upset at the idea.

"I thought I was doing okay for a bit," I say honestly. "Then I had this incident now that makes me wonder what I'm even doing here."

Matt wiggles across the bed to me and lays beside me. "What happened?" he asks with a serious tone.

I laugh. "A young woman told me she was a fan and approached me. I just... freaked out. Literally. I ran away from her. Then I was scared to even use the elevator." I think of my antics, running to the third floor, and wave my hand in the air. "I'm seriously a lunatic."

He kisses the side of my face. "I'm sorry," he says.

I shake my head. "You couldn't have done anything for me." Although that's not true. He could have been there. He could have been present for my event and book signing. I want to tell him that. I could yell at him for not being there. Instead, I take a deep breath.

"I hate your publisher," Matt says, staring at the

ceiling. "Look what they're doing to you. Making you do this after what you went through. How many more do you have?"

"A few next week," I say, shaking my head. I sigh. "I have to talk to Vanessa about them. We're supposed to meet tonight. They won't be anywhere near as large as today's though. Signings at smaller bookstores."

Matt shakes his head. "I really hate your publisher," he repeats. "If it's too much, don't do it, okay?"

I look at him with a thin smile. "So how do I get paid?"

"Who cares about that?" Matt says. "You've made enough money. Maybe they won't even stop the royalties. It could have been just a threat. Let me talk to them for you."

I shake my head. "Probably not a good idea. You'd tell them how much you hate them."

Matt laughs. "Fine, a lawyer then. We hire one to consult with. We have grounds to sue them if they stop paying you. Look what working with them has done!"

I shake my head. "Well, anyway, what did you do today?" I ask, changing the subject. I'm also curious what he's been up to instead of being with me.

"CN Tower," he says with a smile.

I nod my head. That was something we were supposed to do together. We talked about going there and a few other places after the convention was over. Did he somehow forget?

Is he even telling me the truth? I shrug off that thought and my anger.

"That's nice," I say. "How was it?"

He shrugs his shoulders. "Meh. Okay. I don't think you would like it. What do you want to do with the rest of the weekend?"

I want to roll my eyes but don't. I wanted to do touristy things with him but can't now. I'm not sure where we could go that he hasn't been. When I don't answer him, he starts to name a few things we could do. As he rambles on, I think of my interaction with the fan in the hotel lobby. I'm completely embarrassed by how I handled myself.

I roll over to my side and face him. "We shouldn't have stayed at this hotel. It's connected to the convention. Too many fans around. I don't think I can handle it. Maybe we should just go home instead."

"Home? Back to Alberta? Chestermere?" he says with surprise. "Come on. This is like a vacation for us. We need it."

"I don't want to be here, though."

He nods. "I'll look into booking us somewhere else to stay this weekend, okay?"

"I don't know," I say. "I seriously just want to decompress after today at home. Far away from where anybody will recognize me."

"Let's sleep on it," Matt says. "Tomorrow morning, if you still feel like leaving, we will. I'll rearrange the flights and we can go back. If you want to stay and have fun, we can. I'll book a separate hotel."

I sigh. "Okay."

"Perfect!" he says with enthusiasm. "Are you hungry?"

"Starving!"

"There's this great looking steak place at the hotel. Should we check it out? I smell it every time I'm in the lobby and salivate."

"Can we just get room service?" I plead.

He makes a face. "Really? Cut our trip short and not even try the restaurants?" He kisses the side of my face when he sees my expression. "Okay, sorry," he says. "I know you had a hard day. I just wanted to treat you. Celebrate you going through with it. Have some wine. Go for a walk around the city after. It would be romantic." When I don't say anything, he gets it, finally. "Sorry," he says. "Long day. Hard day for you." He gets up from the bed. "I know there's a room service menu around here somewhere."

As he starts to look, I become even more aware of how my anxiety is making things worse between us. I wish I wasn't a writer anymore. I wish I never opened the email from IWriteAlone.

I wish things were better between Matt and me.

"Hey," I say, sitting up from the bed. "Let's try the steak place. It did smell great in the lobby."

He smiles. "Perfect!" he shouts. "Give me like ten minutes. I just want a quick shower."

"Timing you," I joke.

He pulls his wallet and cell phone out of his jean pockets before going into the bathroom and closing the door. I hear him turn on the shower and whistle some song out loud.

IWriteAlone ruined more than just my career. It impacted my engagement to Matt. I changed after what happened to me with the stalker.

Matt whistles louder and now he's singing some song I don't recognize. I look over at his cell phone. I stand up from the bed and walk over to it. I stand over his phone as I contemplate trying to unlock it.

Matt always uses the same passwords for everything. It would be easy to unlock his phone and see what he's been actually up to while I've been working. Has he been telling me the truth?

I'm not even sure what I'd find. He told me he was out being a tourist today, and I know he was, yet sometimes I wonder what Matt does when he's not around me.

I pick up the phone and take a deep breath, lowering it.

I'm supposed to trust my fiancé. Without trust, how can I marry him?

He made a mistake six months ago. He kissed a coworker at a work party. He told me that night when he got home. He hated himself as much as I did that night for what he did. He broke the trust I had with him, but slowly he worked at getting it back.

He told me how much he resented me for pushing back the wedding date for my career as an author. He explained that he felt angry when I spent so much time on my work. I was never available. He even said he was happy that IWriteAlone made me slow down.

That one hurt. I wish he never said that. IWriteAlone ruined my life and hearing Matt say he was happy it happened crushed me. I understood, though, what he meant. All the resentments were piling up inside him and eventually he did something. Something he regretted immediately.

Kissed a coworker.

Some girl from the accounting firm. I didn't know her when I worked with Matt. She was some new girl.

It was just one kiss, and nothing further happened, but Matt was beside himself. He said he understood if I wanted to break it off with him.

At first, I did.

Then I realized how he could have easily gotten away with it had he not told me. He could have kept the kiss a secret. He didn't, though. The guilt ate him up inside.

My fiancé, my future husband, can't keep a secret like that. On some level I love that about him. I believed him when he said it was just one kiss and nothing else.

Despite me telling myself I forgave him, and despite me saying that to Matt, I'm now about to snoop on his phone. Now the guilt is eating me up inside.

Matt turns off the shower and opens the bathroom door, covering himself with a towel. He grabs another towel to dry his hair. He looks at me. "Are you still good to go?" he asks.

I take another deep breath. "Ready when you are."

Matt puts on clothes quickly, and we take the elevator down to the lobby. We enter the steakhouse and are immediately welcomed with the rich aroma of sizzling beef.

My shoes squeak against the polished wooden floors as I step inside. I feel slightly out of place amongst the men in their tailored suits and women in their cocktail dresses. I should have kept on my outfit from the convention. The lighting is low, casting a glow over everything.

Matt tells the host that he has reservations. As we follow her to our table, I'm slightly annoyed that Matt held a spot for us at the restaurant without asking me.

He glances at the plates of food and smiles at me. "This place looks great," he says. He's like a kid in a candy store, only it's beef. He really is in full tourist mode.

The host stops at our table, and we thank her as she hands us menus.

"I saw some guy with a T-bone that looked amazing," Matt says, skimming through the menu. "What are you thinking?"

"No clue," I say, glancing around the restaurant. I can't help but have a feeling of uneasiness. The convention just finished. Readers and fans will certainly be nearby and some likely eating here. I'm not sure how I talked myself into coming here with Matt.

"Sidney?" a deep voice says. "Sidney Meyers?" I turn and a handsome man is staring at me. His jawline is sharp, and his curly hair is styled effortlessly. Whoever this fan is, he's drop dead gorgeous and has a commanding presence about him. "I thought that was you," he continues. I look at my fiancé, who doesn't notice the stranger at our table. He's not interested in a fan's interaction with me, only the steak he's about to order.

"I'm sorry, do I know you?" I ask.

The man laughs. "It's me, Cole."

CHAPTER 5

The handsome man smiles when it doesn't register immediately. When his light blue eyes connect with mine, it suddenly hits me.

"Cole," I say, sharing his smile. "Cole Murphy... Well, how are you?"

He laughs. "I thought that was you. It's been what? A decade?"

"Almost," I confirm. Matt looks at me, waiting for an introduction to the stranger. "Sorry, this is my fiancé, Matt Wilson."

Cole turns to my fiancé. "Nice to meet you, Matt."

"Likewise," Matt says, and they shake hands. "How do you two know each other?"

Cole laughs. "We go back to the stone age together."

I sigh. "We're not that old, Cole. Barely over thirty. We were friends in high school."

"Friends?" Cole says with a suspicious tone. "You don't give me any credit. Technically ex-boyfriend since we dated for an entire month."

I laugh. "Well, three weeks, but still pretty good by high school standards. What are you doing here in Toronto?"

"I've been out here for a little while now," he says. "Do you live here too now?"

"No, just visiting. What are you doing out here?"

I ask, completely interested. I haven't seen Cole Murphy since I was a teenager. I admit I haven't thought about him in years, but he was always a fun guy to be around.

"Well, I'm pre-med. I went back to school late in the game. I have one more year left and next time I run into you randomly, I'll force you to call me Dr. Murphy." He looks back towards a younger woman sitting alone at a table. "That's my girlfriend, Tess." He waves at her, and she shakes her head and shyly waves back.

I smile at the young woman. She's easily six or more years younger than Cole. She's pretty, with long blond hair tied with a ribbon. She looks around the restaurant, and I can tell she's not sure if she should come over and introduce herself or stay in her booth.

If Cole is anything like how I remember, he likely didn't tell his girlfriend where he was going before abruptly leaving to say hi to me. He was so spontaneous. You never knew what Cole would do next. It was something that I found attractive back in the day.

Cole waves awkwardly at his girlfriend again. "Well, I don't want to bother you guys. And Tess is giving me that look that screams 'stop waving at me awkwardly and being embarrassing'."

Matt laughs. "I know that look," he says and glances at me playfully.

"By the way, the steak here is fabulous," Cole says, making a chef's kiss gesture.

"T-bone for sure," Matt says.

"Perfect. I'll leave you guys alone, but hey, it was great seeing you again, Sidney."

"You two have a great night," Matt says.

"It was great seeing you," I say.

I watch him as he goes back to his table and sits

on the same side as his girlfriend, Tess. He whispers something in her ear. She quietly laughs, and I hear a faint snort.

"So, ex-boyfriend?" Matt says, his eyes wide. I know he's kidding. Matt's not the jealous type at all. He's the type of guy who will have a beer with anyone, will talk with anybody, and will always find a way to get along with people.

"Yeah, a long time ago," I say. "He's such a funny guy. Can't believe we ran into him here, Toronto of all places."

I can hear the quiet giggles of Tess as Cole and her secretly talk between themselves, holding hands. It's cute seeing them sit at the same side of the table.

Cole has certainly grown to be a handsome man. His personality may be the same, playful and charming as it was back in the day, but his appearance has definitely improved. When we dated, he was a little overweight. He had braces and bad acne. Now, he could pull off a modeling job.

And he's going to be a doctor. I can almost picture him modeling in tight white underwear, a stethoscope around his neck, wearing an unbuttoned white doctor's jacket revealing his abs that I'm certain he has.

Dr. Cole Murphy, your new patient is waiting for you.

I smile at how corny my imagination is. I glance at Matt, who's still looking at the menu.

"Are you up for an appy?" he asks.

"An appetiser sounds good," I say.

Matt is almost the reverse of Cole. When I first met Matt, he was in a good shape. He worked out often and played a lot of sports in bar leagues with his friends.

When we became serious, he says he got

'comfortable' as he called it. Soon after we started dating, he gained over twenty pounds. He's still a handsome man. The extra weight makes him slower in all facets of life though. Especially in the bedroom. Matt used to be able to take me for an adventurous ride whenever we got into the sheets. It's a bit of a dull ride these days – that is, when we actually engage in sex.

My mind runs wild again. Dr. Cole is the attending physician. Next patient please. I imagine Dr. Cole Murphy taking off his white doctor's jacket, revealing his chiseled chest and large shoulders.

"You want escargot?" Matt asks.

I shake off my thoughts. "Uh, yeah. That sounds great."

Tess snorts louder this time, catching the attention of another table nearby. "Sorry," Cole says to the man at the table. "My girlfriend is not allowed at comedy shows because she's too loud." The older man smiles back, and Tess smacks Cole in the shoulder. "We're also not allowed out in public," Cole says, "due to how violent she is." Tess rolls her eyes playfully.

Matt laughs at the interaction and looks at the menu. "You're right," he says to me. "He's a funny guy."

I look at Cole. He's saying something to Tess and she's looking at him with sultry eyes. I wonder what the two are talking about. Cole looks away from his gorgeous girlfriend, and for a moment, his smile drops from his face as he looks directly at me. We gaze at each other for what feels like a lifetime before he turns his head back to Tess.

The waitress comes up to the table. "Can I get you any drinks?"

Matt nods his head. "Water for now, but can we

order the escargot?" The waitress says she'll bring it right out.

From the corner of my eye, I see Cole stand up from his table and saunter towards me. He smiles as he approaches. Matt reciprocates his expression.

"I'm so sorry to bother you guys again," Cole says. "Listen, it's been such a long time since I've seen you. I never see anybody from those times since I came out here. If you want, I'd love for you to join us at my table."

"Uh…" I say, not sure what to tell him. Part of me wants to. The other side feels it's a bit weird. I'm on a date with my fiancé and my ex-boyfriend wants to make it a double-date? Then again, it was a long time ago. Clearly, we have both moved on.

Matt looks at me, trying to decipher how to respond. I can already tell he's interested in sitting with them. He's a social guy and has been on his own the whole week out here being a tourist.

"No pressure, guys," Cole says, putting up his hands. "I don't want to ruin your date or anything."

Matt shakes his head. "No, no, you're not." Matt looks at me again and I can read his face so well. He's mentally trying to force me to say yes.

"Sure," I say to Cole. "That sounds lovely."

"Perfect." Cole smiles at my fiancé first. "Shall I show you to your table, then?" He gestures towards Tess, who again is rolling her eyes at her boyfriend's humour.

"It's okay to say no to him," Tess shouts out. "He may not be used to hearing it, but his sense of humor only gets worse the longer you talk to him."

Cole turns to us with a wrinkled grin. "She's actually correct. But I'll buy your drinks."

Matt laughs. "Done!" He starts to head towards

Cole's table, and I reluctantly follow.

Tess shakes both of our hands when we approach her. "Tess Simmons," she says. Matt and I introduce ourselves. We sit at the table across from them and suddenly it's quiet. I have no clue what to say. Cole breaks the silence.

"It really is great seeing you again," Cole says. He stares into my eyes for a moment, and I'm captivated by how blue they are. I remember being completely infatuated by his eyes when I was younger.

"I'm happy to see you again, too," I say.

CHAPTER 6

"So," Matt says looking at the couple, "how did you two meet?"

Cole smiles at Tess. "Take it away, dear. Tell them our amazing love story."

She rolls her eyes playfully. "We met online."

"Ah, yes," Cole says. "Truely a romance made in heaven. We talked online for quite some time before I worked up the courage to ask her out, and... she said no."

Tess snorts again. "You always tell people that."

"I want people to understand the rejection I've been through," he says. "It's not easy being me."

Tess looks at Matt. "He's older than me, as you can tell." Cole squints his eyes at her. "I wasn't sure about him at first. I mean, he's certainly different from any man I've dated."

"By that, she means that I'm really annoying," Cole says.

"Well, there's that," Tess says, smiling back.

"Thankfully, my heart wasn't completely broken after she tore into it, and I eventually asked her out again, to which she reluctantly agreed. And almost four months later, we live together now."

"Congratulations," Matt says. "That's great."

"Thanks," Cole says. "We're staying at her folks' place."

Tess sighs. "It's their vacation home," she says. "We don't live with my parents. You don't have to share that it's not mine."

Cole laughs. "Right. Well, it's not our home. Someday I hope to own a house like it, though. It's right on the lake. Really beautiful. I did well hooking up with a rich girl."

Tess sighs again and looks at me. "Was he always this terrible?"

"In high school, he was even worse," I joke.

The waitress brings us our drinks and Matt thanks Cole for buying them.

"So," Matt says, taking a sip of his wine, "why did you two break up?" He looks at me and back at Cole. I can feel my cheeks turning red. Why does my fiancé have to go out of his way to ask awkward questions? I remind myself it happened over a decade ago and it's not a big deal.

"Good question," Cole says, looking at me wide-eyed. "What exactly happened?"

Before I can say a word, Tess speaks up. "She obviously came to her senses." Matt laughs, followed more loudly by Cole.

"Well," Cole says, looking at my fiancé. "We just weren't really into each other, I think. I don't think we had that spark romantically. We were better off as friends."

"How did you two become friends?" Tess asks.

This time I answer. "He was my English tutor."

Matt raises his eyebrows. "You struggled in English?" He laughs at the irony.

"She did," Cole says and looks at me. "I saw the ad your mother put on a bulletin board at school and called. I was looking to make some extra cash. I started working with her on her grammar and spelling."

"You got me into reading too," I say with a wide smile.

Cole's face drops momentarily before a smile returns. "That's right. You hated everything about English class. I got her to read a few chapters of this old true crime book, and she was hooked."

"What book was it?" Tess asked.

I smile at her. "*In Cold Blood*, by Truman Capote."

"So, what do you do now?" Cole asks. "I'm dying to know what your life is like now. Obviously, you've moved on to more mature men." He smiles at Matt and my fiancé laughs.

"Actually, I'm a writer," I say.

Cole's mouth drops. "No way. Really?"

"She's being modest," Matt says. "She's a *New York Times* bestselling author actually."

Cole looks at me and smiles. "That's incredible. What's the book that you wrote?"

I clear my throat. "I've written a few but the bestselling one is called *My Life as a Killer*. It's a psychological thriller told exclusively from the villain's point of view."

"An entire book written from the bad guy's view?" Cole asks. "The killer?"

"Yeah, it's very different, but many readers love it."

Cole slams the table. "Well done, Sidney."

"Thanks," I say, giving a shy smile.

"That's wonderful," Tess says. "Cole's always wanted to write a book. I guess you'll have to ask your old friend for pointers."

He gives a thin smile in reply. "I'm not very serious about it. My manuscript is several years in the making but only a handful of chapters. Not anything like you."

"Don't give up," I tell him. "I'd be happy to help if you want to reach out. Email me anytime." Matt looks at me, and I realize what I said. "Or give me your number. You can always text."

"Thanks," Cole says.

"Do you still read a lot?" I ask. Cole was such a bookworm back in the day. He would always have his nose in something.

"Unless you've written a medical textbook, I haven't read it," Cole jokes. "But now I'll have to read yours." He looks at Tess a moment and back at me. "You're not here for the convention, are you?"

I nod my head. "I was actually a speaker at it."

Matt coughs. "Being modest again. More like a keynote speaker. The main event of the convention."

"That's incredible," Cole says, and looks at Tess. "I wish I'd known. We would have gone to watch you speak." As he smiles at me I try to hide my disappointment. Matt knew how much of a big deal my event was and was off spending time alone in Toronto instead.

Cole raises his glass. "Cheers to you and your success, Sidney."

The four of us raise our drinks and take turns clinking our glasses with each other. When Matt and Tess strike their glasses together, he stares at her a little longer than needed before looking back at me.

Cole clears his throat. "Now I not only need to buy your book, but I need an autograph. You're a celebrity!"

"Stop," I say with a laugh. "Still the same."

Cole drinks his beer. "Well, I suppose you should be buying our drinks now, since you're just as loaded as Tess's parents. If it wasn't for my tutelage, maybe you wouldn't be a famous writer."

Matt laughs. "Next time, if there is one, drinks will be on us."

"Now that's a plan," Cole says. Matt and him clink their drinks together again. "Only we have to have proper drinks. No wine or whatever you're drinking there." Matt laughs.

Tess clears her throat. "How long are you in Toronto for?"

"Just a few more days," Matt says. "Back to Alberta soon."

"Maybe sooner," I say, giving Matt a look.

Tess nods when Cole raises his eyebrows, full of expression. "Hey, why don't you stay with us? We're at this beautiful house that's right on the lake." He looks at Matt. "It's top notch. Beautiful place."

"With you?" I say taken back.

"Cole," Tess says playfully. "They're on vacation. They don't want to spend it with us."

Cole makes a face. "Just an idea. Well, the invite is there."

CHAPTER 7

After dinner, Cole gave both of us a bear hug goodbye, while his girlfriend shook our hands, apologizing for Cole's behaviour. We shared a few more pleasantries before leaving the restaurant. Matt and I had started towards the elevator when he asked if I'd be up for a walk before calling it a night.

It was dark outside, and while part of me worried about the interaction I had with the fan in the lobby prior, and wondering if it would happen again, dinner was just so much fun. I had a lot of energy after dining with Cole and Tess.

A walk sounded great.

As we stroll along the streets of downtown Toronto, Matt reaches out and grabs my hand. I give a thin smile as we walk in silence. Just a few moments ago, both of us were nearly as loud as Cole was. His energy was infectious.

Now we're completely deflated when he's not there and all we have is each other.

My cell phone rings in my pocket. I let go of Matt's hand and look. "It's Cole," I say. I read his message out loud. "Had a great time catching up and meeting your lovely fiancé. Now you need to invite me to the wedding. I know you declined, but if you want to come by the lake house for dinner or something, you're welcome to. Just let me know if you change your mind. If not, I'll see you in about fifteen years at another random place. Take care."

Matt laughs. "What a fun guy," he says. "He just has this energy about him, doesn't he? Was he always like that?"

I nod. "Oh, yeah. He was always loud and trying to entertain the entire room."

Matt looks at me and holds my hand tighter. "Doesn't really seem like the tutoring type. I'm surprised."

I laugh. "Well, he wasn't a very good one. He did help me find my love for reading though."

"Doesn't really seem like a doctor either," Matt says. "I always assume they're stuck up and too serious, but Cole has such a fun sense of humor." He looks at me. "I'm surprised you only dated him a few weeks. I know that's weird to say, but I can't help but think about it."

"We were better off as friends."

"You keep saying that," Matt says, an eyebrow arched as we turn around a corner. "You never exactly explained what that means."

"Cole can be fun, in doses." I laugh. "He never was a serious guy. He always was 'on', and it could be obnoxious at times. I think I just got tired of it."

A memory flashes of Cole when I told him I wanted to break up. His beautiful light eyes filled with rage immediately as he began yelling at me for being two-faced. He cried out that I was a liar. He was able to flip from happy to angry at a moment's notice. It was the only time I saw him that way, but it scared me.

"Good looking guy too," Matt says. It's a weird comment for him to make. Matt isn't the type to talk about men's appearance. When I look over at him, he's staring at me, waiting for an answer. I wonder if part of him is somehow jealous of a relationship that took place for three weeks when I was a teenager.

"Yeah," I say. "He was a bigger guy in high school. Lost a lot of weight from the last time I remember."

"His girlfriend is beautiful too," Matt says, staring off into the street.

This time I stare at him. "Yeah. A lot younger than Cole too."

Matt rubs his hands together and breathes into them. "A bit of a breeze tonight."

"We could go back to the hotel."

He shakes his head. "No, that's okay. I miss walking with you like this. Remember when we first started dating? We would walk for hours and just talk."

I smile at the memory. "We'd always start with a Starbucks and grab another coffee on the way back."

Matt smiles. "Even when we first met at the accounting firm, we would go for walks on break together. Now, here we are. Still together. Still walking."

He stops suddenly and grabs my hand. "I love you," he says softly as he leans in for a quick kiss.

His lips are soft and cold at the same time. I'm not sure if it's from the breeze or my own confused feelings, but his kiss lacks warmth of any kind.

I think of Cole and Tess at the restaurant. The two of them sat on the same side of the booth and looked lovely together. You could instantly tell from their aura and from their kisses that they were both in love.

If a stranger watched Matt and me kiss, would we look anything similar?

Their love is new, though. Mine is stale. Slightly bruised after what Matt did with his coworker at the work party. I wonder how Matt felt after he kissed his coworker. Did he have the same enthusiasm as Cole did with his girlfriend?

"I love you too," I say quickly. I grab his hand and turn away from him, forcing our walk to continue.

My phone rings again, breaking the tension.

"Cole really wants us to come to his lake house." Matt laughs.

I read the message and sigh. "It's not Cole," I say. "It's my editor, Vanessa."

I read her message. "You didn't show up for our meeting. This is completely unacceptable. I've been waiting for more than fifteen minutes. Please meet me at the conference hall where we planned to. We need to talk."

"Is everything okay?" Matt asks.

I sigh again. "I messed up. I have to go back to the hotel. I was supposed to see Vanessa for a late meeting."

"You have to leave, again?" Matt says with a face of disappointment. "We just started our walk."

I turn and look at the hotel. "It's only a few blocks away. Let's just go. This shouldn't take long. You can come with or stay in the room."

Matt sighs. "No, that's okay. You go. I'm going to keep walking."

"Matt," I plead. "I want to spend time with you, but I just have this last commitment."

"That's fine," Matt says. "We've got the rest of the weekend, right? Or are we leaving?"

Leaving is what I'd like to do but I don't tell him that. "We'll stay in town for the weekend. Have fun, okay? So, are you coming with me?"

Matt kisses me and takes a step back. "Go to your meeting. I'm not done walking. I'll catch up with you later." He turns and walks down the block. I watch him and take a deep breath, wondering how different things are between us.

I wonder if Matt and I ever looked like Tess and Cole.

CHAPTER 8

As I walk into the room attached to the conference hall, Vanessa is waiting for me. She's sitting at the table I was at for the signing, texting on her phone. When she sees me, she lowers it and gives me a wide smile. I hate it when you see a superficial expression like the one she's wearing. It's obvious she's not very happy, especially after the texts she just sent me.

"Hey Vanessa," I say. "I'm so sorry about coming late. I—"

"Don't worry, Sidney. I'm glad you came. I was worried you might not show."

I take a deep breath. It's a fair comment. I didn't want to be there in the first place.

"So, how was it today?" she asks. "I know it wasn't easy."

I nod. "Not so bad," I say. For a moment I think about sharing my incident in the hotel lobby with the fan but stop myself. Vanessa is my editor, not my friend. She works for my publisher. And what they care about is money they've invested in me, not me in general.

Vanessa smiles, this time a little more genuinely. "That's good. Well, the company wants me to go over how your new book is progressing."

I'm pretty sure I stop breathing as she says the words. The answer is zero. Nothing. Nada. Not a single sentence. Sure, I tried to write many times. It was all garbage, though. It was almost as if I forgot how to be an author.

Vanessa takes out a clipboard. "Actually, we should start by confirming your dates for your next signings. I have them all here for you." She opens the clipboard and hands me a sheet of printed dates and locations. "They're all the places we reviewed over the phone. I just want your commitment now to double check there's no issue."

I take a deep breath and look at the name of bookstores with times and dates next to it. I can feel myself getting lightheaded as I do. I'm not even sure I read anything clearly as I confirm with Vanessa that it won't be a problem.

"Great," she says. "So, how's the book going? The mother-in-law story."

I take a deep breath before answering. "I'm changing things up a bit. I'm thinking of doing something else."

Vanessa stares at me in disbelief. "We agreed to the mother-in-law story. Stories about in-laws are hot right now. That's what our domestic thriller audience wants. You should have talked to me before changing lanes, Sidney." She catches her breath. "Well, what are you writing now?"

I look around the room as if the answer is written on the concrete walls. "I'm thinking about writing a story about a couple." I think of Cole and Tess. "This couple gets invited to a secluded cabin by some new friends that they just met."

Vanessa's eyes light up. "I always love secluded settings. You got my interest. What exactly happens?"

"A lot. I'm still fleshing out the main plot points."

Vanessa gives me another look. "You're still

plotting?" When I don't answer, she looks away. "Just how many words have you written?"

"Nothing yet," I say. "I'm still—"

"I'm not sure what to say here, Sidney." Vanessa shakes her head. "I mean, the success of your book is amazing. I thought you'd be so motivated to keep your momentum going. We've already extended your deadline by six months. The publisher wants a finished manuscript in less than five months. What am I supposed to say to them?"

I lower my head. "I... can get it done."

"Can you?"

At that moment, there's something about her face that bothers me. It was because of the success of my book that my life's been a mess for the past year. It's because of my publisher that I put off my marriage and now things with Matt and I are... I'm not even sure what they are. But it's not perfect.

I think about what Matt said before. I don't have to be an author anymore. If it causes me this much stress, I don't have to put up with Vanessa. I don't have to put up with my readers. I don't have to do signings. I don't have to do anything.

"Vanessa," I say in a stern tone. "After what happened to me, I don't like your tone. You know what I went through. And what did you do about it? What did your company do about it?"

Vanessa stands up from the table and puts the clipboard down. "There was nothing we could do about your stalker. The police couldn't do anything about it. How could I or the publisher do something?" She takes a step back. "And we offered you therapy. You declined. I'm more than happy to help with that again."

"I don't need therapy," I say. My blood is boiling now. I'm on the verge of yelling.

Vanessa lowers her head. "What are you saying here, Sidney?"

I take a deep breath and think of Matt. "I don't want this anymore. The signings. Writing. I'm done... I'm done!"

Vanessa stares at me for a moment. I wonder if I look as intense as I feel right now.

"Please be kind to return the advance my company provided you for the second book, then," Vanessa says. "If you're not doing the work, you shouldn't be paid."

I'd like to tell her where I'd like to put her company's money right now but bite my lip. I watch Vanessa as she leaves. I stand alone in the room now, white walls surrounding me. The only item that remains is the table, the large poster of me smiling while holding my book haunting me.

I take my time going back to the hotel room. I worry that I'll run into Vanessa on her way to the same elevator. Thankfully, I don't. Thankfully, I don't run into any more fans either. All I want to do is lay down in the bed and wish this bad day never happened.

When I walk up to the door, it's partially open again. I wonder if Matt's back from his walk. I open it and realize something much worse.

Someone has been in my hotel room. The sheets, pillows and my clothes are scattered across the room. My laptop bag is open. The laptop is smashed on the ground near it.

I step inside, taking in our trashed room and my stuff everywhere. When I move, I hear a crunch at my feet and see ripped paper. It takes me a moment to realize it's copies of my book that's been shredded to pieces.

but unless one is pointing directly at your room, and of course, there isn't one, there's not much I can do. All I can do is recommend you stay somewhere else, like your fiancé suggested."

"What a surprise," I say, shaking my head. "The police are useless, again. Something terrible has happened to me and you are powerless to do anything, again."

He looks at Matt who again apologizes for me. The officer nods and walks out of the hotel room.

I turn to Matt. "I bet he wouldn't even check the camera footage if there even was a camera pointed at our room." I sigh.

"I'm sorry," he says. He hugs me tightly. "I'll figure out where we can stay the night, okay? I'll talk to the hotel and get us checked out. Let's just start with cleaning up this mess and pack up. We're leaving. Don't worry."

"I just want to go home," I say again.

Matt lowers his head. "I know you're freaked out. I am too. Let's try and make the best out of it, though."

"Easy for you to say." I stand up from the bed. "None of your stuff was destroyed by the freak who did this." I realize in fear that the hotel room door is open. Anybody could just walk in if they wanted. I quickly shut the door, pushing it hard to ensure it locks properly before putting on the dead bolt. "I want to leave here. Get away from all the readers or anybody who knows about my books. Let's just go home."

Matt sighs. "This may be our last vacation until the honeymoon, whenever that actually happens."

I cover my face. "Can we not do this right now? The last thing I want is to fight over our wedding again, please."

Matt shuts his mouth and I'm thankful he doesn't open it again with more fighting words. After a few moments of silence, he tries to rationalize with me. "Well, if you don't want to stay in the city and there's no flights, where should we go?"

I look around the room. I stare down at the pages of my shredded book by my feet.

Matt grabs my cellphone on the bed beside him. "I guess there's one place we can go."

CHAPTER 9

I sit in the hotel room bed and try my best to maintain my cool. Matt sits beside me and pats my leg.

"It's okay," he says.

The policeman standing over us jots a few notes in his notebook. "So, you're an author at this convention, from out of town? You believe you were the target of this incident?"

I nod my head. I point out all of the items of mine that were destroyed, tossed about or broken. I pick up what's left of my book as an example to show the officer. "Whoever did this definitely had me in mind."

Matt clears his throat. "None of my things were targeted. My suitcase was open, but nothing was really taken out. Just sorted through."

The officer nods his head. "I see." He looks at me. "You came back to the bedroom at approximately nine, correct?"

"That's right," I say, nodding. "I had a meeting with my publisher right before."

The officer jots down something in his pad, then points at Matt. "And you came back soon after?"

He nods. "I was out for a walk. When I got back, I found my fiancé frightened and her belongings everywhere. She had already called the police before I came."

The officer lowers his notepad. "Do you often go for walks at night alone in downtown Toronto?"

Matt looks at me with a thin smile, then back at the cop. "Sometimes, I guess. We were walking together but Sidney had to leave to get to her meeting on time."

"I see," the officer says. He paces around the room and notices a pair of panties on the ground. "I agree with you, Ms. Meyers," he says, looking at me. "I think you were the target here. Seems like a weird thing to do, shredding your books like this. Do you have any inclination about who may want to target you like this?"

"No," I say quickly. "I don't see who would."

"No poor interactions with a fan at the convention, today or another day?" the officer asks, putting the pen to his lip. "Anything out of the ordinary for an event like this?"

I think of the woman in the lobby. I ran away in terror from her when she approached me. I think about why I was scared to begin with. There was a reason why I never wanted to come to this convention. There's a reason why I was scared to leave my home for some time.

IWriteAlone2009.

I haven't opened my email account in forever, though. I wonder if I did, would I find a nasty email from my stalker again? Would there be a recent one of an image of my hotel room? A caption that read that they did this to me? Even after all this time, could IWriteAlone still be taunting me? My popularity as an author has only grown since my last email with her. This is a popular convention, and many readers know of it.

"There could be someone," I say to the officer. I glance at Matt, who looks at me, confused.

"No," Matt says. "Hun, it's been forever since we

heard from them. This has to be something different."

"Who are you referring to?" the officer asks.

Matt looks at the officer. "My fiancé had an internet stalker."

"I see," the officer says.

"It was more than that," I say. "They followed me in real life too. They took pictures of where I went for coffee, of me in public and my house. They did it through email, though, and I never saw them. I have no clue what they look like or if they're a woman or a man for that matter. IWriteAlone2009 was the name of their email address."

The officer writes in his pad. "And when was the last time you heard from this person?"

"Over nine months ago," I say. "I stopped checking my emails completely. I was getting too upset."

"Why's that?"

I look at the cop, trying to maintain myself. "Because the police—nobody would do anything to help me!"

Matt wraps his arm around me and holds me tight. "It's okay. I'm here. It's okay," he repeats. He looks at the officer. "Sorry, this is a touchy subject. It really had an impact on Sidney."

The officer nods. "Do you think it may be worth checking your emails to see if there's been any more from them? Maybe they are still writing to you."

"It may be worth a shot," Matt says.

"I can't look at it," I say, shaking my head. "I won't."

Matt takes a deep breath. "I'll check for you, okay?"

The officer puts the notepad in his pocket and fixes the gun belt around his waist. "I have what I need for the report. If you log into the email and find anything, let me know."

For a moment, I worry the officer will leave. "Wait, is that it? What do I do now?"

The officer looks at Matt and back at me. "Have you reported this to the hotel as well yet?"

Matt nods his head. "I did. As soon as I came to the room, after calming my fiancé, I called the front desk. They told me to talk to them after the police arrive."

"Did they say what they can do?" he asks.

Matt shakes his head. "I don't suppose they're going to pay for any damaged belongings of ours, but I'm sure they will at the very least give us a new room."

"New room?" I repeat. "There's no way I'm staying at this hotel another night. No thanks."

Matt pats my leg. "Okay, we can check into another hotel or something."

I lower my head. "I just want to go home. I don't want to be anywhere near this convention. I'm just done!"

Matt tries to calm me. "Okay. What do you want to do?"

"I just want to go home," I confirm. "That's it."

"There's no flights home tonight. We'd have to wait at the airport. I'd rather put my head down on a pillow."

The officer interrupts us. "Here's my card," he says. He stretches out his hand to me, his card firmly in it, but I don't grab it. I look away from him and my fiancé.

Matt grabs it. "Thanks," he says.

"If you find anything else out, let me know," he says and turns to leave.

"That's it?" I say to the officer. "Let me guess, you won't do anything about what happened tonight?"

The officer turns to me again. "I'll be honest with you. There's very little we can do here. I'll be checking in with the hotel to see what camera footage they have,

CHAPTER 10

We're outside the hotel waiting as Cole rolls up with a beat-up Honda Civic that looks as old as his girlfriend.

Matt holds my hand and grabs our luggage. "It will be okay," he says reassuringly. I grip his hand.

"Thanks for understanding," I say. "I know you didn't want to leave."

"It's fine. Now I get to find out more about my wife-to-be from her ex-boyfriend," he says playfully.

I roll my eyes as Cole steps out of the car and opens his trunk. "Good evening," he says, tipping an imaginary hat. "Your chariot awaits."

Matt whistles. "And what a chariot."

Cole looks at his car and back at my fiancé. "Well, tuition isn't free. Some day I'll own a Lambo. Until then —" he gestures at his car, "—this will work." He grabs both of our luggage and shoves it hard in the trunk. One of the case's corners is sticking out.

"We could put that one in the backseat," Matt says. "With Sidney."

"It's no problem," I say. "Really."

"Nonsense," Cole says, waving us off. He attempts to wiggle the bag around. "It's like a game of Tetris. You just have to figure out how it fits in." He attempts to shut the trunk, but it bounces back. He shoves the suitcase hard until the corner is now only slightly out and slams the trunk down. Even he looks surprised when it fully closes. "See," he says proudly. "Now, let's hit the road. We have at least an hour before we get to my place."

I sigh. "You drove an hour to get us tonight? I'm so sorry. I wish I would have known. We could have figured something else out."

Matt looks at me. "You didn't want to spend the night here," he says, confused.

"Well, we could have gotten a taxi or something," I say.

"Nonsense!" Cole says. "You're our guests. I wouldn't care if I had to drive for hours today." He looks at me. "It's worth it. And after the night you had, it's the least I can do. I can't believe someone broke into your room like that. But try and forget about it for the next day or so. The lake house will help with that. Wait till you see it."

Matt smiles. "Thanks again, man. So, you drove all the way home and then back here to pick us up? Now you're driving an hour back?" He looks at me and back at Cole. "What can I say? Thanks."

"Well, I do expect a five-star review on our vacation rental page," he says with a laugh. "And you buy the first beer run."

"Deal!" Matt says, laughing.

I can't help but join them. I haven't seen Matt like this in some time. The way he talks to Cole, you would think they've been friends for some time. They are already beyond chummy.

Matt opens the front passenger door and steps in. As I go to the back, Cole beats me to it, opening it wide. "And for the lady." He gestures. As I climb inside, I smell a faint aroma of beer coming from Cole. I thank him and he closes the door.

As we begin our drive to the lake house, the reservations I had about calling Cole and asking him to stay at his place are entirely gone. Never would I have thought that I would be staying at the house of a former boyfriend with my fiancé.

I sit in the back quietly as Cole and Matt chat about some of their shared interests. It turns out that Cole may be a bigger movie lover than Matt is. The two go back and forth about movie trivia from horror and thriller movies.

"Have you ever watched *Misery*?" Matt asks. He turns his head to me. "Sidney doesn't like it because it's about a writer forced to write." He laughs.

Cole stares out the windshield. "You know that one's been on my list for some time to check out, but I haven't."

Matt shakes his head. "Just when I thought you were the coolest guy, too. You can't be a thriller fan without watching *Misery*. Maybe we can find a way to watch it this weekend."

Cole gives a thin smile. "Sorry, mate. No television."

"What?" Matt asks. "No T.V.?"

"Nope," Cole confirms. "No cable. Barely a cell phone signal on the best of days. But we do have a hardwired internet connection… which doesn't work great but does its job. The lake house is kind of secluded, you could say. It's beautiful, though. You'll love it."

"What do you do for fun?" Matt asks.

"We mostly talk to each other," Cole says. "Read."

Matt shakes his head in amazement.

"Sounds wonderful," I say.

"It is," Cole says, glancing at me in the rearview mirror. When our eyes meet, I turn my head and look outside. As we get out of the city, the busy streets begin turning into dense woods. We pass fewer and fewer houses. Cole slaps Matt's leg. "All Tess and I do is talk and, well... you know."

Matt shakes his head and smiles. "So that's the secret to a happy relationship."

I turn my head and look at my fiancé, wondering what he meant by that comment. Was there something personal attached to it? We haven't had sex in some time. I can't even remember how many weeks it's been now. Is this Matt's way of throwing a verbal jab my way?

He already threw a sucker-punch at me with his *Misery* joke. I look outside again at the bright full moon hiding behind the dense trees in front of it. A chill runs down me and when I turn back, Cole is looking directly at me in the mirror.

"Everything okay back there?" he asks.

I give a thin smile. "Yeah, I'm just enjoying the ride."

Cole nods.

Matt takes a deep breath. "I think Sidney's still a little shook up after what happened."

Cole nods and glances at me again. "Of course. Who wouldn't be afraid? Don't worry, though. You'll love it at our place. Nobody's around for miles. Nobody bothers you." He looks up at the road and gets awfully close to a black Ford truck that's ahead of us. I almost feel the urge to hold onto something for the impact when Cole slows down and slaps his horn.

"Come on!" he shouts. He tailgates the truck again. "Why are you in the fast lane?"

Matt's smile that's been plastered on his face since entering the car begins to fade. "You can just go around."

Cole ignores him and hits his horn again at the truck. "Move!" he shouts. He pushes down on his horn continuously until the truck gets the hint and changes to the other lane. "Finally," Cole says. He drives up slowly, taking a moment to look through the passenger side window at the driver of the truck. For a moment, I worry what will happen next, until Cole turns back to his windshield again and the road ahead.

I look out my window and see the driver of the truck, a woman wearing a blue cap, has her hand on her chest. She's obviously frightened. Cole continues to drive as if nothing happened.

There's a bit of silence until Matt breaks the tension. "A bit of road rage there, eh buddy?" Matt laughs and Cole joins him.

Cole looks at the rearview mirror. "I'm used to driving in Toronto. Tess hates my driving too."

After the incident with the truck, the energy inside the car changes. Matt and Cole are still chummy but not as talkative as they were before. I've seen Matt lose it at others while on the road, but there was something about Cole that seemed different, rageful even. His eyes switched from jovial and welcoming to murderous. And over what? Not speeding as fast as he was?

As we continue to drive, the forest seems to surround us entirely, almost consuming the car. I haven't seen a house in over ten minutes.

Suddenly Cole turns down a gravel road. He drives for several minutes, and I still don't see his house. I'm starting to wonder if he even owns one or is just driving us to the middle of nowhere.

I hate my imagination. It always jumps to the worst imaginable situations. It's the curse of being a domestic thriller writer. Everyone has bad intentions in my mind.

"You guys really do live out in the middle of nowhere," Matt says with a thin smile. He takes out his cell. "Well, I have two bars out here."

Cole nods. "Surprised. Usually we don't have any."

As we continue down the gravel road, I spot a string of dull light ahead. The lake house finally begins to emerge from the trees. The place has a rustic elegance to it, with its weathered wood siding and large windows. Cole said the house is on the lake, but with no lighting around us beside from the porch, it's hard to see the water.

"Home sweet home," Cole says.

On the dimly lit porch is Tess, standing by the front door. She waves and smiles at us as we park outside.

CHAPTER 11

"Please, help yourself," Tess says as we sit at the dining table together. "Once I found out you guys were staying over, I quickly rustled a little something up."

I look over at the charcuterie board. Piles of sliced meat and cheese surround a bowl of black and green olives. "Looks great."

Cole kisses the side of her neck, making her flinch. "She comes off like a good hostess but wait till you see her other side."

Tess gives a thin smile and shakes her head. "Not true." She grabs a glass on the table and a bottle of red wine. "Care for a glass?"

Matt and I both thank her. Matt takes a sip and compliments Tess on choosing such a fine wine.

Cole smiles at Matt and shakes his head. "Matt, I thought you were the coolest guy until I found out you were a wine snob."

Matt smiles. "I appreciate a fine vintage." He grabs the bottle and examines the label. "And this one is quite expensive. Thanks again."

"No problem," Tess says.

"It's her father's wine," Cole interrupts. "I suppose we should be thanking him too." He opens the fridge. "Matt, can I grab you a beer too? Or are you happy with your girly drink there?"

Matt looks at me a moment and back at Cole. "I'm okay."

Cole grabs two bottles of beer from the fridge. He twists off the caps with his other hand before sliding one of the bottles across the table. "You really do need to try this beer though. Got it from a local brewery."

Matt thanks him. Cole sits across the table from Matt. He kisses Tess on the side of her face and looks back at Matt. "Give it a taste. No fancy swishing around your mouth or smelling it now. You just drink."

Matt has a thin smile and grabs the bottle. He looks at the label. "Donkey Ass?" he laughs. "They actually call it that?"

Cole laughs. "I didn't name it. I just drink it. Cheap and does the trick."

Matt takes a small sip. "Not bad. A little hoppy for me, but good."

Cole nods. "Tomorrow we'll go for that beer run. On you." He laughs, pointing at Cole.

"That's right."

Even though Matt and Cole are both smiling, I feel tension. I can't place what it is. It's almost as if Cole is subtly making digs at my fiancé. I look away from them and notice Tess is doing the same. Our eyes meet and I give a thin smile.

"So, this is your folks' place?" I ask.

Tess nods her head. "I wish it were mine, but yeah."

"How long are you guys staying here?" I ask.

"Forever." Cole laughs. He takes a long drink. "Well, until whenever her old man kicks us out, I guess."

Tess sips her wine. "They said we can stay for as long as we need. They're out of the country right now anyway. They're on a safari in Africa for the next few months."

"Safari?" Matt repeats. "Some life your parents live."

Tess nods. "They vacation often."

"It really is a beautiful house," I say.

"Thanks so much, Sidney," Tess says.

Cole spits out some of his beer. "It's not like you decorated it, Tess, or had to work for any of it." He wipes his mouth. "Being born into your family doesn't mean you did anything to deserve this."

Tess looks away from him to the wall before turning back to me. "Do you guys swim?" she asks, changing the subject.

"Matt's a fish," I say.

Matt nods in agreement. "We didn't bring anything, though."

"You can always borrow a pair of swim trunks from Cole," Tess says. She looks at me. "I have an extra bikini too."

"Sounds great," Matt says, answering for me. He grabs a piece of deli meat from the charcuterie. "Can we get the tour?"

"My pleasure," Cole says, standing up, his beer bottle firmly in his hand. "Follow me." He walks to a door beside the edge of kitchen cabinets. "This is to the backyard balcony. Just wait until you see the lake tomorrow. You can't see anything out here at night, but it's a sight." He walks past another door. "This leads to the basement. A whole bunch of boxes and other useless stuff her parents hoard, but there's a wine cellar." Cole makes a clicking sound with his lips. "Sidney, Matt, help yourself to the cellar. Help yourself."

Tess looks at Cole for a moment. I wonder if she feels the way I do. Cole seems off. The incident with the truck driver was just weird. His breath smelt like alcohol when he picked us up at the hotel. How much has he had to drink tonight? Is he drunk? Why does he seem so agitated all of a sudden? He seems like a different person to the one we had dinner with.

Cole waves for us to continue the tour as he walks into the small living room. I confirm for myself that there is no television. I notice a family photo above the fireplace. A larger man with a thin mustache smiles beside a woman in a white dress. Below them is a young girl with short hair, smiling awkwardly for the photo. The girl has light brown hair.

Tess stands beside me. "My parents," she says, "and me when I was a bit of a tomboy."

Cole stands on the other side of me and wraps his arm around my shoulder. "She was quite hideous as a child, I must say. She's definitely had a glow-up as an adult." The stench of beer is stronger now on his breath. Tess shakes her head at his comments.

As Cole begins to walk upstairs, he takes a step, nearly missing it and losing his balance. "I guess the bar needs to cut me off," he jokes.

I look back at my fiancé and wonder if he can read my mind right now. How many drinks had Cole had before coming to pick us up at the hotel? Has he been drunk the whole time? The issue with the truck on the road. He comes off slightly irritated right now too.

"We just have the two bedrooms upstairs, an office, and the bathroom," Cole says. He passes by a room. "That's ours." He points at another. "This is the bathroom, and the office is the room next to it." He stops in front of a door and opens it. "And your room." He opens it and gestures for us to walk inside.

The room is small, with a twin bed taking up much of the space. A small window is near a closet. It would be cozy if not for the unsettling picture on the wall of a dishevelled man biting into a child.

Cole smiles at me. "I had to look it up. It's a print of a painting that's apparently famous. It's called 'Saturn'." I look at the child's face screaming as the man's teeth dig into its chest. "Weird, right?" Cole says. "It's supposed to represent fear or jealousy... whatever."

Matt looks at the painting and turns to me in disgust. "Some taste Tess's parents have."

Cole smiles at me. "I don't usually like art, but this one speaks to me."

CHAPTER 12

I stare at the wood paneled walls in our room, trying not to lock eyes with the painting on the wall. As I toss and turn, Matt is breathing heavily into his pillow, nearly asleep. I'm always jealous of his ability to nod off wherever he is without much issue. I sleep in a hotel room instead of my bed and I can't get a good night's rest.

Matt could doze through a war and get amazing sleep.

I turn again, taking some of the comforter with me.

"Can you stop that?" Matt says into his pillow. "What's wrong?" He turns on his side to look at me. "Are you still upset about the hotel?" He yawns.

Still?

It just happened. How can he be so nonchalant about an intruder breaking into our room? Sure, he was upset with the hotel staff as we checked out. He complained about the bedroom door not locking properly. One of the young customer service agents at the desk asked him why Matt didn't report the issue with the door when he noticed it. That got Matt really upset. Thankfully Cole came soon after to pick us up.

As I've been tossing and turning since we climbed into this small double bed, I've been trying to figure out why I can't sleep either.

Part of me still wishes we'd just gone home on the

next flight. There's a hotel beside the airport. I could have possibly slept better there knowing I'd be on one of the planes leaving the next day. I should have said that. Instead, I let what Matt wanted to do decide for us.

Part of me is still upset about that. The other half of me is wondering what the hell I'm going to do with the rest of my life now that I've ruined my author career. Not too many writers can go crawling back to their publisher after the meeting I had today.

Maybe it felt good in the moment to tell Vanessa how I felt, but was it worth it?

"I'm okay," I say. I roll over to my back and stare at the ceiling. "So, I have sort of a career update for you."

"What happened?" Matt says, placing a nearly limp arm around my shoulder. "You never told me what went on with Vanessa."

I take a deep breath. "Well, it seems like we may need to get a lawyer, and I may need a new job."

Matt sits up in bed. I tell him what happened with Vanessa, and I explain how she demanded the advance back that was paid to me.

"Everything's going to be okay," Matt says, blankly staring at the wall. Part of me wonders if he's somehow falling asleep with his eyes open until he turns to me. "I know how hard it's been for you lately. I know. We'll figure it out. You can always come back and work for me. My company would love to hire you back in a minute, especially now that you're famous."

I sigh. "I'm not even sure what I want." I turn to my side.

That's not entirely true. I think about what life would have been like if IWriteAlone never messaged me. I think about what would have happened if I married Matt last year, instead of putting it off. I wonder what my life would be like if I never found out about Matt and his coworker.

I think about how upset Matt was today with the hotel staff. I compare that to Cole with the woman in the truck.

"What do you think of Cole and Tess?" I ask.

He nods. "Fun couple. Can't believe this house. Imagine living in a place like this everyday."

I breathe in deep. "Wasn't it weird how angry Cole got at that truck driver today?"

Matt yawns and nods his head. "I've seen worse. When I was a kid, my dad would flip the bird at many drivers with me in the car. I still remember how angry my mom would get at him when he did." Matt laughs.

"He seemed a bit off before we went to bed too," I say.

Matt raises his eyebrows and pulls the blanket from me, taking more of it for himself. "Just too much to drink, I guess." He yawns again. "Let's just get some sleep, okay?"

I fidget under the sheets and my leg leans against his. "I still think maybe we should leave tomorrow."

Matt rubs his face. "I thought we said we'd stay the weekend."

I breathe in deep. "I'm feeling out of it. I don't know. I still just want to go home."

Matt sighs. "We said we would stay the weekend with them already. I don't want to be rude."

I feel a flash of anger come over me. "I swear, Matt. The only thing that matters in this relationship is what you want."

Matt groans. "Fine. Let's just enjoy the day tomorrow. If you still feel like leaving, just give me the face and we'll make an excuse to leave."

"Face?" I repeat.

Matt smiles. "Give me that not so subtle face you have when you're not happy." When I don't laugh, he turns to my side. "Okay. Tomorrow. You tell me, and I'll make up an excuse and we can go."

Matt kisses my forehead and turns back. I continue to stare at the ceiling, wondering why I'm so uneasy. I almost feel physically sick, but don't have any symptoms. I think about the feeling I had when I stepped on the shredded pages of my book in the hotel room. I think of Cole's face when he lost his cool at the woman driver.

Finally, I hear the sounds of Matt's heavy breathing, bringing me back to the present.

I'm not sleepy whatsoever. I wish I could be the light switch that my fiancé is and be as restful as he looks. Instead, I'm stuck in my head, as usual. I suppose that's what authors are always like.

I remind myself that's not even who I am anymore. I'm no longer going to be a writer. So what does that make me? Who am I? I'll be restarting my life in my thirties. I feel like a teenager in senior year desperately trying to figure out what they'll do for the rest of their life before school ends.

I slide out of the bed and take a moment to look at my fiancé before opening the bedroom door. The door creaks so abnormally loud that it makes me jump. I look at Matt, but he's still sleeping. Like I said, a bomb could go off and he'd wake up wondering why everything around him was destroyed.

I don't bother closing the door out of fear of the noise it would make. I step towards the bathroom when a faint muffled sound stops me. I look down the dark hallway and hear it coming from Tess and Cole's room.

As I take a step down the hallway, the muffled sound becomes louder and more identifiable. Someone's crying. A woman.

Tess.

Part of me wonders why, but then my next step creaks loudly on a floorboard. I nearly gasp and quickly walk into the bathroom and close the door behind me, managing to make only a few more squeaks along the way.

I look at myself in the mirror and take a deep breath. I remind myself whatever is happening in their bedroom is none of my business. I barely know Tess.

I can't help but wonder if she's crying because of something Cole said or did. I run the sink and splash some water on my face. I notice the painting on the wall behind me in the mirror. It's an image of a monkey sitting on a toilet with a wide smile. It makes me grin and I question who chose the artwork in this house.

The painting in our room and now the monkey on the potty in the bathroom. When I leave the bathroom, the sound of muffled crying has stopped. Obviously Tess must have heard me.

I stop outside my room. I can't go back inside just yet. I'm too wide awake. The thoughts of my day and feelings of the past won't let me sleep. I decide to go downstairs. I'll have a drink of water, hopefully get my mind off everything, and when I'm ready, go back upstairs.

I slowly walk down the stairs, and each step makes a different sound as I do. When I get to the ground floor, I go to the kitchen. The large windows in the living room reveal the dark, calm waters outside. Cole wasn't joking when he said how beautiful it was here. The moon, now bright and high in the sky, illuminates the wooden patio that leads to a private beach.

I open the patio door and take a step outside. The night is cool, but the temperature is perfect. I take a few more steps and look out at the water.

It's eerily quiet, though. The only sounds I hear are the short gusts of wind against the trees that surround the lake and the house.

The sound of glass rattling startles me. I turn and see Cole sitting on a patio chair behind me. He stands up and leaves his bottle of beer on the arm.

"Sorry," he says. "Didn't mean to scare you. I thought you guys were asleep."

I catch my breath. "Matt's asleep," I say.

"Tess is asleep too."

That's not true. I heard her crying in her room just now, but I don't mention it. He stands beside me on the patio and leans against a wooden railing, looking out onto the water.

"I never thought I'd end up in a place like this," he says.

"It's beautiful," I say, turning to look at the water with him. "I'd love to find a house like this someday."

Cole nods and clears his throat. "Maybe I'll get lucky and Tess's parents will give us this house when we get married someday... or when they croak."

I try to forget his last comment. "Cole Murphy, getting hitched? She's wonderful, though. I wish you both the best."

"I'd never thought I'd run into you again either." He laughs.

"What are Tess's parents like?" I ask. I'm curious given their taste in artwork.

"I still remember how you'd sneak out of your parent's house on nights just like this, to be with me," Cole says, changing the subject.

I sigh. "Well, I sort of had to. I knew my parents wouldn't approve of me hooking up with my English tutor."

Cole laughs again. "Nope. Definitely not. Especially since I was eighteen and you were fifteen."

"Fourteen and a half, actually," I say, staring off across the dark water.

He raises his eyebrows. "Okay, well, yeah, I would have been furious if I was your dad. I always wondered: did you ever tell your parents about us dating?"

I shake my head. "No."

Cole smiles. "I always thought you had. I mean, you ended things with me and suddenly my job as a tutor ended as well. I just assumed that you said something. I was too scared to find out more."

"I didn't say a word," I say. Looking back at it now, I can't believe that Cole would have ever wanted to be with a girl as young as me. I was completely fascinated by his infectious energy. At first, I thought it was cool to have an older boyfriend. Cole got a little pushy though. He was ready to explore more sexual things that I wasn't comfortable with. He was always respectful when I told him to stop, but that didn't stop him from trying. I ended things before they went any further than passionate kisses in his car.

When my grades didn't improve in English, my father fired Cole. Wasted money. He would have been furious had he discovered the truth, which Cole shared with me while we were dating.

He had no experience in tutoring, as he claimed to

CHAPTER 13

The wind pushes Cole's hair to one side. He brushes it back with his palm and smiles at me as he leans closer. We don't speak. All the talking is done with our locked eyes, waiting for one of us to make the next move.

Cole, of course, makes that decision easily. He smiles as he comes in closer, his mouth only inches away from mine. I know it's wrong, but part of me can't help but wonder what his lips taste like. I remember how sweet they were when I was a girl.

Now, Cole is even more handsome. Charming. Funny. He's got a bad side though, and doing this will change everything in my life.

I grab his chiselled side as we kiss. I can feel my entire body jitter with excitement as our kisses become more passionate. I welcome his tongue inside me, and he brings my body closer to him. I can feel how excited he's getting.

As if a switch is flicked on, it suddenly hits me how wrong this is. What about Matt? The man I'm supposed to marry? Then again, Matt did the same to me.

We're even now.

I can't, though. I'm not that type of person.

"Cole," I say as he kisses my neck. "Let's stop. Let's—"

"No," he whispers in my ear and bites it softly.

While his mark leaves me wanting more, I urge him

have when my parents interviewed him. He likely did just as poorly as I had in high school. He did help me discover my love for reading though.

Something that nobody will ever be able to take away.

Cole looks out at the water and stands closer to me. "So, you being a writer, how much did I truly influence you? You love writing now. I guess that was because of me. Something good happened because we were together."

I turn to look at him and Cole is already gazing at me with his light blue eyes. A gust of wind moves his curled hair. His lips purse as he waits for my response.

I take a deep breath. "Sorry, Cole. I'm getting tired. I should get some sleep. Talk to you tomorrow. Have a good night."

"I will," he says with a smirk.

I walk back into the house, and as I turn to close the door, I see that Cole is still watching me.

to stop. When he doesn't listen, I push him away from me. Instead of Cole, a dark shadow with red eyes looks back at me.

"No," it whispers.

I take a step back as I hear a voice call out from far away. "Sidney!"

I open my eyes, breathing heavily, my face dug into the pillow. I roll over and catch my breath as I take in how bright the room is. I turn my head and notice that Matt isn't in the bed with me, and the bedroom door is fully open.

I also notice the pool of saliva I created on the pillow and wipe my mouth on the blanket in disgust.

Matt is always an early riser. I couldn't stand how much of a morning person he is, especially when we worked together. By the time I woke up, Matt would have already been ready for the day and reading the news online. He'd always warn me to get ready faster or we'd have to take separate cars to work. I thought that when I started working at home as an author, he would have enjoyed not having to wait for me, but he told me he missed it.

I hear footsteps creaking down the hall. I quickly get out of bed and close the bedroom door before I can see their face. I'm not even sure why Matt left the door open like that. It freaks me out knowing that someone could have walked in and seen me sleeping.

While I know Cole, the more I get to know him as an adult, I'm not sure how comfortable I am with him. I certainly was comfortable with dream Cole though.

Dr. Cole is ready to see you. I imagine Cole shirtless in a hospital setting, waving me into an exam room.

I smile at how cringeworthy my own fantasies are.

It's like the setup for one of the sleazy pornographic movies I would see in Matt's browser history.

I get changed and open the bedroom door. Even as I try my best, the door creaks loudly. As I walk down the hall, I hear a familiar laugh coming from downstairs. Soon, another laugh erupts, and someone claps their hands.

When I walk downstairs, I'm greeted by both Cole and Matt as they sit at the dining table.

"That's a true story," Cole says, eating a piece of bacon from his plate.

Matt looks at me. "I never knew my Sidney was like that."

Cole nods his head and eats another piece of bacon. "Your Sidney was something else back in the day."

The idea that my ex-boyfriend and fiancé are talking about me wakes me up faster than coffee can. "What did I do?" I ask with a thin smile.

Cole smiles at Matt. "Nothing at all," he says. "I'm just telling your fiancé all your dark secrets from your past." Matt laughs.

I sit beside my fiancé. "Morning, love," he says and kisses me on the cheek.

"Breakfast?" Cole asks. Before I can answer he stands up and grabs a plate of food from the kitchen counter, placing it in front of me. Two eggs, with a sliced tomato in the center and a piece of bacon made to look like a smile.

Matt laughs. "He made me the same."

"Not hungry?" Cole asks. "Or don't like my culinary presentation? Well, I can make that smile a frown for you." He turns the plate around and the bacon mouth becomes a frown.

Matt laughs at the joke. "Want something to drink?"

he asks. "Cole made fresh squeezed orange juice." He makes a face of delight as he takes a bite of his bacon. "What a life you live here, Cole. Fresh juice, breakfast smiles, and all of this." He waves at the lake outside. Several boats are far out in the water. The sun glitters off the calm surface. "You must feel like a king every day here."

Cole nods his head. "This place is something else."

"Where's Tess?" I ask.

Cole sighs. "Still getting up." He uses his fingers to air quote. "I swear that woman would wake up at noon if I let her."

Matt laughs and points at me. "Sidney is way worse."

"I am not," I say.

Matt, taking the subtle hint, rubs my back. "I know. I don't get you creatives. You take a nap and to you that's work because you're thinking about a scene or whatever."

I quietly take a bite of the tomato nose on my plate.

"What do you do all day if you're not writing?" is one of Matt's most popular questions. Or "Maybe you should get a regular job." He likes to say that one when I tell him how much I've been struggling.

Cole breaks the tension. "You guys will love dinner tonight. Do you like lobster?"

Matt raises his eyebrows. "Yes. Love lobster."

"Dinner?" I say, swallowing my tomato piece. Did Matt not get the hint last night? I don't want to stay another night. The plan was to leave. I stare at my fiancé. He said he wanted me to give him a look when I wanted to go, yet my gaze seems to go over his head as he and Cole laugh on about something else the pair were talking about.

"Cole?" a small voice calls from the stairs. "Can you

come here?"

Cole raises his eyebrows as well. "The queen beckons me." He stands up from the table and walks upstairs to Tess.

I take the opportunity to talk to my fiancé. "I wanted to leave today," I remind him.

Matt takes another bite of his bacon and nods his head. "Right. We will. After dinner."

I roll my eyes. "I thought we talked about this."

Matt nods. "Right. We did. Come on, Sidney. The man invited us to stay for dinner. What was I going to say?"

"Say sorry, but we have to leave."

Now Matt rolls his eyes. "Check in at any hotel isn't until after four in the afternoon. What are we going to do at an airport hotel until then?" He gestures outside. "Just look at that. Cole says he'll get a lunch barbeque going. He wants to go into town to get some things for lunch and dinner. After we eat, you can borrow a bikini from Tess."

"I don't exactly want to borrow someone else's bikini. Do you want to borrow Cole's underwear?"

Matt takes a deep breath. "I'm borrowing a pair of his swim shorts. Let's just do that thing that people do when they're on a trip. You know, enjoy ourselves. Besides, Cole says he'll drive us to the airport after dinner."

"He did?" I say, half amazed that Matt bothered to ask him.

Matt nods. "So let's enjoy today, okay?"

I don't answer him. Instead, I take another bite of the tomato nose. "Is everything okay with Tess?"

Matt shrugs his shoulders while taking another sip. "I don't know. I haven't seen her today."

"I heard her crying last night in her room."

Before I can say another word, Cole walks up to the table, holding Tess's hand. From her tone of voice when she called out for Cole to come upstairs and after hearing her muffled crying last night, I assumed she'd be upset, but Tess smiles brightly at Matt and me.

"Morning," she says.

CHAPTER 14

We pile into Cole's car again. He tells us there's a small town nearby. I sit in the back seat with Tess. She's staring out the window and isn't giving off a talkative vibe today. Yesterday she was somewhat reserved too, but today is much worse. I'm not sure why she was upset last night and what she and Cole talked about before we left, but whatever it is, she must be thinking about it hard.

She's barely acknowledged the fact that I'm sitting beside her.

The aura of the front of the car is different. Matt and Cole have been joking and laughing nearly the entire trip. Their "bromance" continues to thrive.

Matt is an outgoing guy. I knew that immediately when I met him. He's always jovial and looking for a conversation, even if it's with people who aren't talkative, like me. Somehow we've made our relationship work even though I'm very much an introvert.

Cole is like Matt in that way, only multiplied by a hundred. Cole has to be the most enigmatic man I've ever met. He was like this when we were younger, but now that he's older, and more handsome, he has an energy about him that's infectious. While he can be obnoxious at times, his looks help you get over it.

I can tell Matt is having a blast. But I'm ready to leave. Even though Cole can be welcoming and charming, last night I saw a glimpse of what may be simmering under the surface. He came off a little tense. Matt chalked it up to him being intoxicated, but I'm not sure.

I'm happy that this is our last day at the lake house. Although we haven't discussed when we're leaving. Matt said it would be after dinner, but what time will that be? Some people eat as late as nine at night. What happens if Cole claims to be too tired and full from dinner to drive us? Then we'll have to wait another night. I wouldn't want that.

Cole and Matt erupt with laughter over something Cole has said and break me out of my thoughts. I look over at Tess and she's still staring out the window. I suppose she's used to blocking out Cole by now.

Matt looks at the houses passing by. "What's the name of this town anyway?"

Cole makes a face. "Not really a town, actually. More like a tiny hamlet in the country."

Cole turns into the parking lot of a small grocery store. He parks and turns his head.

"Liquor store is just across the street," he says. "Matt, beer is on you, I believe."

He nods in response. "I'm a man true to his word."

"Excellent," Cole says. He leans against his driver's seat and takes out a piece of folded paper from his jean pocket, handing it to me. "Here's a list of what we need for lunch and dinner." He looks at Tess. "You got cash on you?"

Tess doesn't reply but shakes her head while still looking outside.

Cole sighs. "Ugh, okay." He grabs his wallet and hands her a few bills. "That should cover it. Tess and Sidney will get food. Matt and I will get the necessities."

Matt laughs at the corny joke as the two of them open their doors, stepping out.

"Everything okay?" I ask Tess. Instead of answering, she opens the car door and leaves me in the car alone.

By the time I exit and close the door, Matt and Cole are already walking toward the liquor store, laughing about whatever one of them has said. I shake my head, wondering how two adults can get along so quickly. The two are kindred spirits of corny jokes.

Tess puts out her hand. "Here, I'll take the list."

I hand the piece of paper to her and thank her. The bell above the door jingles when we enter the small store. The few rows inside are packed tightly.

I grab a cart and we head down the first aisle. Tess grabs a pack of hotdog buns and drops it in the cart.

I don't know Tess well, but somehow, I know that she's not trying to be rude to me. She just comes off like someone deep in thought.

Tess grabs another item from the list and drops it in the cart, but I stop following her. "Tess, did Matt and I do something to hurt your feelings? Did we do something wrong? Is everything okay?"

In my mind, it's the best way to find out what's happening without targeting her for feeling mad or sad or whatever it is. Maybe if I make it about me, she'll confirm it's not and share more. If I just ask "what's wrong with you?" she'll likely clam up.

Then again, maybe she's not exactly happy that Cole's ex-girlfriend is staying at her house. Even if it was only a three-week relationship when I was nearly fifteen, maybe that doesn't matter to her. It is an awkward situation that I'm not entirely sure why I agreed to.

Tess sighs and shakes her head. "I'm sorry, really. I

know you don't know me. I can't imagine what you think of me. It's not you. You guys are both great. I'm happy to have met you. Cole and I got into a good blow out last night. Nothing about anything you did. We... like to fight."

Tess grabs a pack of hotdogs and whips it into the cart. "In fact, we're really good at it. Fighting is something we both seem to enjoy too much in our relationship. We both just trigger each other... all the time. But then we make up." She gives a thin smile. "The make-up part is the best, although I don't have to tell you that."

I laugh shyly. "Well, we never, you know. I was just a kid when I met him."

Tess watches me a moment more before nodding. "Right."

We turn and go down another aisle. "I'm sorry that I've been a downer this morning. I plan on picking it up. I think Cole and I are on the mend anyway, at least until we put our boxing gloves on again."

"Good. Hopefully we can all enjoy our time together until we leave tonight."

"Are you leaving tonight?" she asks, surprised. "Cole said you were staying until your flight in a few days or something."

I look at the shelf nearby and see a jar of pickles. Remembering it was on the list Cole gave me, I grab it and put it in the cart. "Well, we're not sure, I guess."

Tess lets out a breath. "I hope it's not something Cole or I said or did."

I shake my head. "No, of course not. I'm just exhausted from the convention." I can see from Tess's expression that she's taking it personally. Her face looks exactly how it did on the stairs when she was talking to

Cole. I try my best to change the subject and highlight something they did that was nice. "I'm so thankful that you guys let us stay with you, though. After the break-in at our hotel room, I was a wreck. It took Matt forever to calm me down. I'm so happy you opened the door to your beautiful house for us to stay at."

Tess waves me off. "My pleasure. Besides, now I get to tell people that a famous writer was my guest for a weekend."

Actually, it'll just be for a night, but I won't correct her. Instead, I keep trying to praise things she and Cole did for us, to make it less awkward that we are leaving tonight. "I still can't get over how Cole drove all the way back to the hotel last night, picked us up and then went all the way back to your house."

Tess turns her head and goes quiet again. "Cole wasn't at home when he left to pick you up. He was still in Toronto."

"He was?" I say, confused. I'm certain that Cole said differently.

"Cole and I got into one of our famous fights the night before as well," she says. She looks at the cans on the shelf. She finds the one she wants and places it in the cart. For a moment, our eyes meet. "We got into a bad fight after dinner with you guys. It was so bad that I took an Uber home. Cole stayed and I don't know what he did.... probably drink," she says, tilting her head.

It makes sense now. I could feel tension last night with Cole's behaviour. He must have still been amped up from the fight. I'm still surprised, though, that the pair fought. At dinner, they were both so happy. They appeared so in love. If I'm being honest with myself, I was jealous. They sat on the same side of the booth. Their hands were all over each other. They looked like they both couldn't wait to get home and rip each other's clothes off.

Suddenly I think of my hotel room. I remember how it felt stepping over the shredded pages of my books.

"So Cole never came home until after he picked us up?" I ask.

Tess nods. "When I found out you guys were coming, I was happy. You seem like such a great couple, and we don't have many guests."

"And you don't know where Cole was after the restaurant?"

Tess nods again. "He stormed off into the street after our fight. He didn't seem to care how I was going to get home." She sighs. "Sorry, I still get pissed off just thinking about it. We fought last night too so hopefully you didn't hear us."

I shake my head. I truly didn't hear a word. If the two were fighting, they did it very quietly.

"Cole can be so loud when he's upset," Tess says. "Me though?" She laughs. "I'm like a mouse. You wouldn't hear me at all." She tightens her bottom lip. "So I know you wouldn't have heard me, but if you heard Cole, I'm sorry." She takes a deep breath. "That's why we don't have many people sleeping at our house."

Tess turns her head, but I can see her wipe her cheek. There's something about her in this moment that hits me. She's so vulnerable and her trying to conceal it makes it even more fascinating to me.

There's something ironic about her. Cole and Tess are so different. Cole is so loud and obnoxious while Tess comes off more delicate and inward thinking. The couple would make great characters in a book.

I try not to think about that. I hate how my brain

works. I could be witnessing something tragic and think about how great of a scene it would be to write.

I pat Tess on the back. "I'm sorry," I say.

"You've done nothing wrong," she says.

"I know, but I feel like we're invading your space or something. I feel bad. You probably didn't even know we were coming to stay with you. And after the fight you had, I'm sure you'd rather have that time to make up with Cole."

Tess nods. "None of it was my idea, it's true." She breathes out. "And I'm sorry about what will happen." Her words make me catch my breath. Did I hear her right? What did she mean? Before I can ask her, she hurries down the aisle.

CHAPTER 15

With a quick pace, Tess goes down the aisle and stops at magazine stand. On a shelf beside it are some books. She grabs one that I recognize immediately.

"This one is yours, right?" she says with a smile, showing me my bestseller, *My Life as a Killer*. Of course, she knows it is, but I nod my head shyly.

"Yeah, that's mine," I say.

She tilts her head. "Well, you have to do me the honor and sign a copy for me. Like I said, I need proof to show that a famous writer stayed at my place. My parents will be even more thrilled that I'm hosting celebrities at their house."

I laugh again. "Okay, I'm not that big of a deal. I'm not the type to be recognized when I go out places. Hardly a celebrity." I grab the book from her. "Of course I'll sign a copy though. I don't have a pen on me." I look around the grocery store towards the cashier.

Likely they would have one. Before I ask, Tess reaches into her purse and pulls out a blue pen. "I'm always prepared for autographs." As I start to sign the book, Tess claps her hands. "Thanks."

I hand her the book back. "Now you have to pay for it." I laugh.

She smiles. "Now I have to read it too."

I wave her off. "Don't worry if you don't. My own

family doesn't even read my books."

From the corner of my eye, I see a woman staring at us, behind Tess. I glance at her but try not to make eye contact. The woman's expression is so intense. I'm worried if I look at her, she will direct it towards me.

The woman starts to walk slowly up to us, and it hits me that she is making that face directly at me.

"How dare you?" the woman says.

I feel like I've been struck by lightning when my brain makes the connection. It's the woman who was in the hotel lobby. The woman that asked for an autograph but instead of giving her one, I ran away as if she was a monster.

I open my mouth but can't find the words.

The woman from the lobby finds them easily. "I asked you for an autograph and you ran away, making me feel like some freak! Now you're here giving them."

"Uh..." I manage to say.

"I'm sorry but who are you?" Tess asks.

"Screw off," the woman says. "You got your autograph."

"She's my friend," Tess says. She points a finger at the woman's face. "Please leave us alone. Stop harassing us."

The woman stares at Tess a moment before taking a step back. "Whatever," she says. She looks at me. "This is how you treat your readers." She scoffs. "I was your biggest fan."

As she says those words, I cry inside. I can't help but think about the first email that IWriteAlone sent me. I can't stop myself from thinking about the many emails that followed.

The woman storms off but looks at us one more

time before leaving the grocery store.

"What a whacko," Tess says, shaking her head.

I wonder if she's from this town. "Do you know her?" I ask.

"Never seen her before," Tess confirms. She turns to look at me. I can feel my hands trembling. I try to calm my nerves as Tess grabs my hand. "Are you okay?" she asks. "You're so pale."

I'm not able to answer, but I managed to nod my head. Did that woman even have a cart or groceries with her?

CHAPTER 16

Now it's me who's quiet in the car ride back to the lake house. My hands are no longer trembling, and I must not look so pale anymore because not even Matt is asking me if I'm okay.

Although if I was still pale and looking unwell, he likely wouldn't have noticed given how much he's into the conversation he's having with Cole at the moment. The two of them are laughing like idiots in the front seat.

I notice Tess glancing at me every so often. I try to ignore her. I don't want to talk. I don't want to say how I'm feeling. I just want these emotions to leave. I want to leave.

I just want to go home. I want to go to the airport hotel, find a way to change our flights and go home. I don't care what it costs. I don't care what Matt says.

I'm done. I'm checked out.

What are the chances that I ran into that woman again? Does she actually live in that small town? How many people live there?

Soon after my encounter with the mystery woman in the lobby, my hotel room was destroyed. Could she be my stalker?

Why do I keep assuming the IWriteAlone has something to do with my hotel room?

It could all just be coincidental. All of it. Sure, the

woman could live in this small town and be a fan of mine. Well, likely not a fan anymore.

A hand grabs mine. I look over and Tess has a worried expression. "It's okay," she whispers to me.

There's something about her compassion in the moment that calms me. I nod but don't say a word.

I let go of her hand and continue to look out the window at the trees and dense brush. Every so often I catch a glimpse of the lake.

My thoughts continue to run wild until Cole turns onto the gravel road to the lake house. As we get closer, I take out my cell phone. I don't have any reception. No wi-fi. Nothing.

I want to leave. I'm not sure I can stay until after dinner. Something inside me is yelling for me to run home. Hide in my house.

The convention was a mistake. I should never have come.

Matt was right. I've learned my lesson the hard way. I thought I could handle this, but I can't.

Matt and Cole are smiling as they talk to each other as I try to interrupt.

"Matt," I say calmly. When he doesn't answer, I raise my voice. "Matt!"

He looks at me in shock. "What?"

"Do you have any bars on your phone? Can I use it? I want to look something up."

Cole answers for him. "You won't be able to use the net out here on your phone," he says. "The office upstairs has internet. You can use the computer if you want. There's no password to log in with the guest profile."

"Thanks," I say. My hands are clammy as I hold them tightly together.

When Cole parks outside the house, everyone takes their time to exit the car. I anxiously wait to get inside. Cole opens the trunk and grabs a case of beer. Tess grabs a few grocery bags.

Matt looks at me. "Hey, are you okay?"

Finally, my fiancé manages to notice that I'm not *okay*. I've been anything but okay, but I don't tell him that. Not in front of Cole and Tess.

"I'm not feeling good," I say. "I'm going to rest in the room."

Matt gives me a worried expression. "Rest? We're not here for long. Cole's going to start a BBQ and we can go for a swim. Let's just, you know, have fun."

"She's not feeling good," Tess says, speaking up for me. "She said she felt off in the grocery store."

Matt turns to me. "Are you sick?" He puts a hand to my forehead to check.

Thankfully, Tess comes to the rescue again. "Go ahead, Sidney," she says. "Rest and hopefully you'll feel better for lunch."

I thank her. Matt turns and starts talking to Cole as I enter the lake house. Usually, the beauty of the view would have my attention, but right now I just want to use their computer.

I want to search for the next flight out of here. I want to go back to my house as soon as I can.

I can feel my pulse quicken as I hurry up the steps. As I walk down the hallway, I open one of the doors and realize it's Cole and Tess's room and not the office that I entered in my haste.

I try to catch my breath. I need to calm down. Is it possible to have a heart attack at my age? I try to reason with myself. Why am I so worked up?

Over what? So what? I ran into the woman from the hotel lobby again. Why am I losing it? My hand begins to tremble again.

I think of Vanessa, my editor. She offered me therapy a long time ago. I should have taken it. Reacting the way I do to the smallest of situations is not natural. I know that, but when will I do something about it?

I can feel my pulse slow as I take deeper breaths. I'm about to close the bedroom door when I notice a stack of books on the nightstand. All of them I recognize.

There have to be four or five books piled together and all of them are mine. I take a step into the room and slowly walk up to them, looking at the titles.

When I met Cole and Tess at the restaurant, he said he had no clue that I was an author. Now I find a stack of my books in their bedroom?

I pick one of them up. *My Life as a Killer*. There's a fold in the pages about a quarter of the way through the book. Have they been reading my books? On the nightstand is a man's watch and sunglasses.

Cole is reading my books? When I met him, he said he had no clue that I was a writer. Did I misunderstand what he said?

I think about what Tess said at the grocery store as well. Cole didn't drive home like he said he had. He made a big deal of telling Matt and me how he drove all the way back to his house and back to the hotel to pick us up. That wasn't true, though.

I think of how I found my hotel room. The intruder scattered and broke my things. My books were torn to pieces. My laptop was broken beyond repair. This can't all be a coincidence.

I leave the bedroom and close the door quietly.

Despite my best effort, the door squeaks. I catch my breath as I open the door to the office.

I quickly sit at the desk. The computer is already on the log-in screen. There's an admin and guest profile. I click on the guest profile and it slowly loads.

This computer has to be the slowest I've ever seen. If I had my laptop, I'd already be searching for flights. I can't imagine how long it will take for me to find what I want.

There's a browser already open when the profile loads. I click on it. It takes what feels like forever for the page to show. It's a Google search. I'm about to erase the search to look for flights when the words on the screen stop me.

Someone searched my name. My author profile image is looking back at me. It's the same picture used for the banner at the conference. There's a second tab beside it. I click on it and it's another Google search. This time the search was for "Author Sidney Meyers stalker."

There's a forum chat that's highlighted. I click on it. The screen loads an online thread that's all about what happened with IWriteAlone. Somehow fans on the internet knew about it. They didn't mention IWriteAlone's email, but they talk about the stalker.

I lean back in my chair and wonder who searched for my name and the stalker.

CHAPTER 17

There's a last-minute flight tonight back to Alberta. I just have to find a way to get to the airport. I don't care if Cole drives us, or like Tess, I take an Uber back to Toronto, but I'm leaving.

It took me some time to calm my nerves again after finding my books on Cole's nightstand and the searches on the computer.

Now, I just have to talk to Matt. We need to leave. I don't trust Cole. There's more going on here than I know.

This all can't be a coincidence. Inside, my stomach is turning. A voice is not just yelling inside me but demanding that I leave here immediately.

I hear footsteps coming up the stairs. My heart stops until Matt pops his head into the office and smiles at me.

"Feeling better?" he asks.

"We need to talk," I say in a hushed voice.

"What?" he says, confused. Before I can explain, Cole walks up behind Matt and rubs the top of his shoulders.

"My swim trunks are in my room," Cole says as he walks past us.

Matt looks at me. "We're going to go for a swim after lunch. You want to come?"

I take a deep breath. I think about whispering what I want to say to him, but Cole yells out to Matt and he leaves.

I shut the office door and quickly go back into the guest room. I hope that Matt will take the hint and come into the bedroom to talk more.

We need to talk, I said clearly. It was in a low voice, but still. He'll come inside the bedroom and when he does, I'll tell him we need to leave immediately. No fun swim time with his best new buddy, Cole. No hanging out in this house for another moment.

There's a flight back home and a handful of hours from now to get to the airport. The plane will leave today, and I want to be on it.

Unfortunately, Matt didn't get the hint. I can hear Cole and my fiancé chat as they walk past the guest room and down the stairs, the creaking getting more distant.

I cover my face in defeat. My heart is still racing as I try to figure out how I'm going to tell my fiancé I want to leave without it being so obvious.

As I breathe in deep, I ask why I'm so nervous and scared at this moment. So what? I found a stack of my books on a nightstand. Not exactly something to freak out about.

Then there were the searches on the computer about me. I was frantic when I saw it, but could Cole or Tess be curious about my career as a writer?

I remind myself that Cole told me he never knew I was a writer and that he went home and back to pick us up at the hotel last night. Those were both lies.

There was also the intruder in my hotel room.

Do I really think Cole was the one who destroyed our room? Why would he? What purpose could he have?

He was the one pushing for me to come to the lake house. Why? Did he want to have me in a remote place, where I could be most vulnerable?

I always assumed that IWriteAlone2009 was a woman. In my head, she was. What if I was wrong? What if it was Cole all along?

My heart is beating out of control to the point that I can feel my pulse in my lips. I take several deep breaths.

All of my thoughts seem so outlandish. Unreal. I can't trust myself to think rationally anymore. How did I become this way?

I know the answer. IWriteAlone.

After a few more long breaths, I stand up from the bed and leave the guest room. I slowly walk down the steps and can hear Cole and Matt talking outside on the backyard patio. I go through the patio doors and Matt smiles at me. He's sitting at a table close to Cole as he starts the barbeque. The two of them laugh about something as Cole opens a package of hotdogs and tosses them on the grill.

Tess is sitting at the other end of the table, looking out at the lake, sipping tea.

"How many do you want?"

I take a deep breath, trying to calm myself, but can feel my heart beat faster again. Even the beautiful scenery of the lake can't stop me now.

"How many do you want?" Matt laughs.

I turn to him. "What was that?"

Now Cole joins in the laugh. "How many hotdogs? I'll assume two. I mean you're a skinny one, Sidney, but if you're anything like Tess, it will be more than one, even if she doesn't admit it."

"Two's good," I say curtly. I sit beside Matt. I put my hands together and they're clammy again, just how they were at the grocery store.

"So," Cole says, taking his tongs and turning some

of the hot dogs on the barbeque, "Tess let us know about the crazy woman at the grocery store." He looks at me. "That is just intense. Are all your readers nuts?" He looks at me, staring, and waits for my response. Yesterday his light blue eyes were mesmerizing. If I could have, I would have snapped my fingers and turned my fiancé's eyes to his color just to look at them all day.

Now it's different. His look gives me the chills knowing that I've discovered his lies.

"She's had other crazies before," Matt says to me.

"Really?" Cole says, turning another hot dog. "What did they do?" Instead of looking at Matt for an answer, he stares at me again.

At that moment, I can't help it. I know there's something not right. I feel like my gut has been trying to tell me ever since Cole picked us up yesterday at the hotel.

"You should know," I say coldly.

Cole's permanent smile vanishes from his face as he realizes I'm talking to him. "Sorry, what?"

"It was you who destroyed our hotel room, wasn't it?" I say, raising my voice.

Cole looks at Matt a moment and back at me. "You think I broke into your hotel room?" Now I have Tess's attention as she takes her sunglasses off and looks at me.

I stand up from the table. "You told me you never read any of my books, but you have. You have a stack of them in your room."

"You went into my bedroom?" Cole says, surprised.

I ignore his comment. "You searched up my stalker on your computer." Cole raises an eyebrow at me and again looks at Matt as I continue. "And you said you drove all the way to your house and then back to the hotel to pick Matt and me up, but that was a lie. You stayed at the hotel, didn't you?"

Cole looks around as if to understand why I'm zeroing in on him. "I did."

I nod, knowing I'm right. "You broke into our room after we turned down your offer to stay here."

Cole laughs nervously. He looks at Matt again. "This is what? A prank or something?"

Matt doesn't answer. The look of disgust is plastered on my fiancé's face that he's trying to hide with his hand. "I'm... I'm so sorry, guys."

"Ask him why he lied, Matt," I demand. "Ask him."

Tess leans in. "I don't understand."

Cole laughs again. "She thinks we destroyed her hotel room." He shrugs. "For what reason, I don't understand yet."

"To get me to come here," I answer.

Cole shakes his head. "Okay, you got me. My plan was for you both to come here and—" he grabs a hot dog with the tongs and wiggles it at me, "—feed you fatty food and take in some nice scenery." He gestures out to the lake.

"IWriteAlone2009," I say in a low voice.

Cole peers at me. "What?"

"IWriteAlone2009@gmail.com. That's you too, isn't it?" I grab Matt's hand. "We need to leave now."

Matt whips his hand away from me and shakes his head. He looks at me and covers his face again. "I can't believe you're doing this right now. All I wanted was a nice weekend."

I realize he's not going to see what I do.

"She had a hard day," Tess says. "That woman at the grocery store grilled her. She was frightened the whole car ride home." She looks at me. "It's okay, Sidney."

I swallow my own spite and find myself the center of attention as all three of them stare at me.

"Why did you lie?" I say to Cole as I continue to try and make sense of everything. He shrugs. "Why do you have my books?"

"I bought them at the convention," he says. "After dinner, I went there and bought a few. I was curious after you told me you were a writer. I saw your face on some ad near the restaurant saying you were the keynote speaker. I wanted to buy some of your books." He looks at Tess. "You know, support a writer friend. Well, old friend." He looks at Matt. "Maybe not a friend now, I guess. Sidney... I... And the searches. Well, Matt told me about the stalker. I wanted to know more. There wasn't any information online though. Matt said you had a hard time writing after the stalker started bothering you."

Cole stops laughing. His happy face that was etched on him was gentle now. Cornering. He's wondering what the hell am I talking about, and I'm realizing he's right.

Matt has the same look, pleading for me to stop, but I continue.

"What did you do after we left the restaurant?" I ask Cole. "I know you didn't go home with Tess. What happened?"

Cole looks crushed. Even though nobody touches him, he looks physically hurt. "Sidney, you actually think I broke into your hotel room?" When I don't answer, he glances at Matt again. "Okay, well, here it is. After the restaurant, Tess and I got into a fight. She left. I stayed at the bar at the hotel. Had some drinks. Bought some of your books after," he says, pointing at me. He drops his arm back to his side. "And I was on my way home when I got your text."

I turn to Matt. He looks completely disgusted. I know he's going to ream me out later for this.

"It's okay, Sidney," Tess says. She stands up and places a hand on my shoulder.

I sit back down on the chair. All the anger in my face drops. I probably look just as disgusted with myself as Matt does.

"Why did you two fight?" I ask. I look at Cole and then at Tess.

Tess takes a deep breath. Cole shakes his head.

"That's no one's business," he says curtly.

"I am so embarrassed," Matt says, finally joining the conversation. "I can't believe her." He looks at me. "Seriously, Sidney? You're coming off like a psycho."

"She's been through a lot," Tess says, sticking up for me. "It's okay, Sidney. Really. I get it."

"I still don't," Cole says.

Matt stands up from the table and shakes Cole's hand. "Thank you for letting us stay the night and for the meal you had planned, but I think we should just go."

Cole makes a face. "I really thought we were having a fun time, guys. I really don't know what to say."

I cover my face with my hands, hoping to hide my own disgust with myself. Suddenly I remember what Tess said to me at the grocery store.

"Why did you tell me you were sorry for what you would do to me?" I speak.

Matt sighs. "And she's still going. Sidney, let's go. Stop embarrassing me and these people!"

I ignore my fiancé and look at Tess, my eyes beginning to water. I'm not crazy. I heard what Tess said. "At the grocery store you said to me you were sorry about what will happen to us. What did that mean?"

Tess looks down for a moment before meeting my eyes. "I meant it as a joke. Cole's a big idiot. I know he was going to keep saying a lot of dumb jokes to try and charm you both."

Cole raises the tongs in his hands. "I am charming." He lowers his hand and looks at Tess. "And pretty dumb."

"Let's pack our bags," Matt says. He turns to Cole. "I'm sorry again, man, really. Don't worry, though. We won't ask you for a ride. You've done so much. We'll figure something out."

Cole scoffs. "Guys. Let's not do this."

Tess pats my shoulder. "It's okay, really. This was just—"

"A misunderstanding," Cole says, finishing her sentence.

I look at Matt and for a moment our eyes meet. I can tell how upset he is. Upset is the wrong word. He's pissed off. He's probably wondering what kind of basket case he got engaged to. As Matt apologizes to Cole and shakes his hand again, I clear my throat.

"Sorry," I say. I put a hand to my chest. "Really. I, ah, had a moment. After what happened with the—you know, life's been hard."

"A *New York Times* bestselling author?" Cole says amused. "Sounds terrible." Tess gives him a look.

"I'm just as embarrassed with myself," I say.

"It's okay," Tess tries to reassure me.

I nod my head and look at my fiancé again. This time Matt is regarding me sympathetically.

"Really, sorry," I say to Cole. "That was one hell of an accusation to throw at you."

Cole clicks the tongs in his hands. "Well, what, you're traumatized after that stalker. Makes sense. I'd be too."

I look at the barbeque and the blackened hot dogs that are being burnt because of me. I give a Cole a thin smile. "Actually, I'll take three hot dogs."

CHAPTER 18

I sit in the beach chair, watching the scenery. It's beautiful here. Truly breathtaking. Several sail boats are further out in the water. The only thing ruining the scene is the playful banter between Cole and Matt. The two are obnoxiously loud as they play soccer on the beach.

"Goal!" shouts Cole as he kicks the soccer ball between two rocks which they're using as their makeshift net. Matt shakes his head in disappointment as the two continue to play.

"Aren't they something," Tess says, as she lies on the chair next to me. I thought she had gone to sleep. With her dark sunglasses on, I couldn't tell.

"Yes, they are," I admit. I haven't seen Matt connect like this with someone in some time. He has many friends in Chestermere, but I don't think I've ever seen him have as much fun with someone as he has with Cole.

Tess shifts in the chair, fixing her bikini top. A ball flies past us and Tess shouts.

"Sorry! Sorry," Matt pleads as he runs past us. He smiles at me a moment until he notices Tess shifting in her chair. His gaze holds on her just a few moments more than it should before he looks away.

Do men really think it's not obvious when they're checking out a girl? Matt was harmless enough about it, but it was completely obvious and right in front of me.

I try not to get upset at the idea. Just a moment ago, I noticed how beautiful Tess was. Should I blame my fiancé for seeing what I do? He has functional eyes.

Am I really one to talk as well? I noticed how handsome Cole was immediately when he approached us at the restaurant. I've certainly noticed him today.

It's hard not to when he's running around in his swim trunks with no shirt. His body is just what I thought it would be. Chiseled, with an actual six pack.

Paging Dr. Cole. Your next patient is waiting.

This is the same man who I accused of doing terrible things. How can my imagination go from spicy thoughts to him being a monster?

I watch him now as he runs down the beach with Matt, kicking the soccer ball. Sweat is glistening off his chiselled body.

Dr. Cole. Your patient is ready.

I take a deep breath and wish I could remove my brain from my body at this moment. Here I am mentally slighted by Matt checking out Tess when I haven't been so innocent myself.

Cole and Matt tire after a few more goals, Cole getting the better of my fiancé, and lie on the sand together.

It's weird watching them. It's almost like a before and after photo, only reversed. When I first met Cole, he was much larger. Now he has a slim and athletic build. My fiancé's story is the complete opposite. When we first started dating, he was thin. Not very muscular, but very handsome. While he's still good looking today, he's not as eye-catching as he was when we first met.

Sometimes I wonder if we would have hooked up all those years ago if he looked how he does now.

"Are you sure you don't want to borrow a bikini?" Tess asks.

"I'm fine like this," I say. I'm wearing a tank top and shorts, and while the water does look nice, I still feel uneasy about everything.

Just a few hours ago, I disastrously made our day so much more awkward. Now we're hanging out on the beach as if nothing happened.

Lunch was awkward as well at first, but soon after, Cole started making the group laugh and his charm really did wonders in helping me forget what I did. Tess has been quiet, though. We've sat on the beach in our chairs for nearly thirty minutes but haven't said much. I'm not sure what I could say to make things better.

How do I even strike up a conversation after what I did?

I turn to her. "Hey, I'm really sorry about everything today."

Tess shakes her head. "Not a problem."

"I feel so stupid. I'm still embarrassed."

Tess lets out a laugh. "Well, I'd be too, but I hope you stay." She lowers her sunglasses to look at me. "If I had gone through what you did, I'd be the same. Really. I'd probably be a lot worse."

I nod. "Maybe my publisher was right. I need therapy."

Tess gives me a thin smile. "It's not easy to talk about personal things with strangers. I tried therapy once. Didn't really help me much. Maybe I should try again."

"Should we make a therapy pact?" I joke. "If you go, I'll go."

Tess laughs. "Sure. You let me know when you book

a session and I'll do the same." She raises her sunglasses and stares off at the water. "I do have to admit, I think you are completely ballsy. A true badass."

"Is that what I am?" I laugh.

She nods. "I mean, you just tore into Cole. It was funny to watch and see him squirm. I never see him that way. I think I need to learn from you. I'd love to be able to tell him off like that. He's starting to think he's winning all our arguments because they end with me crying."

"What do you guys fight about?"

"All the normal stuff," she says. "I'm a bit of a jealous type. I see red if he's checking someone out. Now that we're living together, we fight a lot about his cleanliness. The man's a literal pig. The house would be a sty if it were up to him. Do you and Matt fight often?"

I tilt my head. "Sometimes, yeah. Lately we've been at it more."

"Why?" Tess asks.

For a moment, I feel like answering. Where do I even start? My career as a writer has ruined my relationship. Matt making out with some office skank ruined our relationship. My being crazy after the stalker has ruined not only my life but our relationship.

"There's a lot between us. A lot of history to unpack."

"Maybe you should save it for the therapist," Tess jokes.

"There was this woman, at his office. Well, it used to be my office before I was a writer. I didn't know this woman, though. Matt told me he kissed her once at a work party. I was really upset about it. I still am."

"That's terrible," she says. She looks at me and I turn away quickly.

"Maybe we need couples therapy." I take a deep breath. "Sorry," I say. "I guess I'm not used to talking about it. Matt's a great man. I know he loves me too, but somewhere along the way, we stopped communicating with each other." I watch my fiancé and Cole talking on the beach. "I don't know, it's like we don't even know each other anymore these days."

"I understand that," Tess says. "Cole is a great guy. Sometimes though, he takes things a little too far. Sometimes he's so warm and fun to be around, while other times he scares me."

I glance at Tess, but she doesn't say more. Part of me wants to ask what she means but I wonder how far I should go with this conversation. I fear what she may say.

I settle for an open-ended question that gets to the point. "Are you safe? Around Cole, I mean."

Tess looks at me. I can see her wide eyes behind her dark sunglasses. "Yeah," she says. She turns over to her side. "I'm going to get some more sun."

"Okay," I reply as she turns fully over.

I stare off into the lake, watching the boats on the water. A jet ski whizzes by. Cole raises his arms and shouts goal soon after they start playing again.

I look back at the lake house. It really is beautiful. Located right on a beach. It's breathtaking.

It would be the perfect setting for a book, I think. The idea was intrusive, almost as if it didn't even come from me. I smile. It's my Muse, talking to me. Sometimes when I think of random stuff, my Muse will scream something at me that's interesting.

Despite not writing a word for a long time, I still hear it inside of me. Sometimes it's loud and wants me to know its presence. Other times it's quiet.

Today it's louder than it's been in a long time.

A remote lake house would be a great setting for a thriller, I agree. I look over at Tess. She would be a great character to write about. A young woman learning to stand up to her abusive boyfriend.

Somehow, in my imagination I've instantly made Cole the antagonist, and one that's abusive at that. I like the idea of writing about the journey a woman takes to find her voice. It would be a scary setting to do it in. A remote lake house. Nowhere to run. I notice the treeline surrounding the lake.

I don't see another house in sight. I imagine someone running through a forest trying to escape. Adrenaline would kick in, I'm sure, but how long could you run through thick brush?

I already imagine a scene in my mind of Cole chasing Tess along the beach outside the lake house. I can see her screaming as Cole chases her, trying to grab her before she escapes him.

But how can she escape him in an isolated place like this? It would be nearly impossible. Especially with no cell service. She would have to outsmart Cole somehow.

I can feel the creative juices flowing in my brain as the dark images of the scene play out in my head. Tess would be a great character. A woman learning to stand up for herself. She finds her courage to face her fears and manages to outsmart Cole.

I shake my head at the idea. Who am I to write about courage? I shake in fear of fans wanting autographs. I've been afraid for so long. I don't even want to be an author anymore because of how scared I am. Who am I to write a character arc like the one I've created for Tess?

If I were to write about her, I couldn't use her actual

name. I couldn't use Cole's either. I'd have to use other names. I reach into my jean pocket and open a Word document on my cell. I put in a few notes for the ideas in my head. Remote lake house. Tess and Cole. Overcoming your fear.

I glance at Tess, wondering if she has any idea of what's running in my mind.

Looking at my phone, something comes over me. I write a sentence. Then another. Soon I've written a whole paragraph. It's the beginning of a book. I can't help but smile. The words are coming so easily at the moment, but my fingers tapping on my cell phone can't keep up with my thoughts.

I stand up from the beach chair. Tess doesn't seem to notice and neither do the boys, who continue to play soccer.

I hurry inside and make my way upstairs to the office. I log into the guest profile and open a Word document. It takes a few minutes for it all to open but when it does, my fingers begin to type as fast as they ever have.

I'm writing word after word. Sentence after sentence. And I'm keeping all of it. I'm not deleting anything. A story is starting to come out of me. I feel more alive than I have in a long time.

CHAPTER 19

As I think about the next scene in my story, I feel a strong urge to find something to make notes on. A separate notepad or piece of paper. Something. It's part of my creative process. I like having something to jot down notes or ideas as I type.

I search through the desk drawers, but most are empty. When I open the largest drawer near my ankle, my eyes widen at my discovery. A silver gun sits on top of a stack of paper.

I wave my head in disbelief as I look at it. Why would a gun be in an office drawer? Who does that?

In Canada, it's illegal to have a gun with no trigger lock. From research I've done in the past, handguns are typically restricted, unless you have a special permit, and even with one, I don't believe you can have one hidden in your office this way.

Was this Cole's gun? Tess's? Or maybe her father's?

I close the drawer quickly as I hear creaks coming from the hallway. A moment later Matt looks into the office and smiles at me.

"What are you doing?" he asks suspiciously. "I told you not to worry. We'll leave after dinner. You don't have to worry about flights right now. Cole's still going to drive us."

I look up at my fiancé with a serious face. "Over

three thousand words," I say in a hushed voice.

"What?"

"Over three thousand words! I just wrote it now. I can't believe it! I mean how long has it been?" I look at the clock. "Almost two hours and I've written that much already. I even managed to edit a little bit of it."

"You're writing again?" he asks.

I nod and stand up from the chair. "Yes! I can't believe it. The story is just flowing out of me. I can't contain it. It's like this book is just jumping out onto the page. I haven't written like this since, well, last year." I smile and look down at the computer. "Okay, I need to save this. Imagine me losing my work by not saving! I haven't written a word in so long and I lose my words by not backing up my work. Ha!" The idea is somehow amusing although that would be a nightmare.

"You're so excited," Matt says confused. "The other night you told me you were finished with being a writer."

"I was… until today." I walk over to him and grab his hand. "I was worried that I'd never feel this way again. I needed this trip."

"That's great," he says. "So what's it about? Your story?"

I don't dare tell him it's about our hosts. "You know," I say. "People getting murdered and yadda yadda."

"Yadda?" Matt laughs. His smile widens when he looks at me. "I haven't seen you this happy in some time. This is great. Now we need to thank our hosts."

Yes, we do, I think. In more ways than one. They're essentially the main characters in my book. Even though the story is coming out of me, I still have no clue how it will end or what will happen within it. I want some kind of a twist. Something big that will make readers' jaws drop. Nothing's come to me yet, but I know it will. It always does. I just need to let the story marinate in my head a little and something will jump at me.

"Let's stay an extra night," I say. "Maybe a few. We can leave in a few days when it's the day of our flight. I could use this inspiration."

That is, if our hosts let us. I did embarrass them and myself not too long ago. I need to stay here now. My Muse is on fire and the story is rolling in my mind continuously. In a few days, I could write a quarter of my book at this rate, easy.

"I know Cole will let us stay," Matt says. "He already mentioned it to me at the beach today."

"Perfect!" I can't contain how happy I am right now.

"Well, if your yadda book makes us even more money, I'll be happy to put off our marriage another year so that we could buy a house like this, on a lake somewhere. You'd be inspired everyday."

I take a deep breath. In an instant, my happy bubble has been popped by his comment. "Why'd you have to say that? We're not going to put off our wedding any longer, okay? I won't do that again."

"I'm just joking," he says with a smile. He leans in and kisses me on the forehead. "I'm happy for you. I am. Congratulations. You've written more than a few sentences!" He makes a *woo* sound. He looks at the computer. "So I guess you're going to be in the office for a bit?"

I go back to the computer and save my document again, ensuring it will be there when I come back. "No," I say to him. "Let's have some fun."

CHAPTER 20

"Chicken fight!" Cole shouts.

Tess smiles at me, slowly circling her fists as she sits on Cole's shoulders. Cole walks through the lake, coming closer to us as he pounds his chest like an ape and shouts.

Matt tries his best to keep me on top of him as he heads toward Cole.

"You're going down, Matthew!" Cole shouts.

"Get her!" Matt shouts at me.

The men slowly walk towards each other through the water, with the women on their shoulders. Both Tess and I shout at each other playfully as we try to push against each other with the aim of knocking the other off the back of their partner.

"Push harder!" Cole shouts as I begin to shove Tess and she nearly falls off. "We're losing!" Cole screams with agony. "Not acceptable!" While trying to keep Tess on his back, he grabs Matt and tries to shake him.

Matt pushes him off, but in the process, I lose my balance and fall into the water. When I come up, everyone's laughing, and I join in.

"Cheater!" Matt screams.

"No!" Cole says with a smirk. "Winner!" Tess jumps off his back into the water and the two high-five. "Belly-five!" Cole jumps at Tess with his abdomen out and knocks into Tess, who falls into the water as well.

When she comes up, she doesn't find his antics funny. "What the heck!"

"Belly high five," Cole clarifies. "I thought you got that." He laughs as he grabs her hand and picks her up. The two have a quick kiss before Tess playfully pushes him.

"Jerk," she says.

"Well," Cole says, patting Matt on the back. "Looks like we won at chicken fighting the last three rounds."

"Twice!" Matt rebuts. "I don't count that last round."

"Okay," Cole says with a silly tone. "Fine. Twice, we won. Obviously team Cole-ess is superior."

"Cole-ess?" I laugh.

"That's right," Cole confirms. "Sounds like Coolness, which we are." He turns to Tess. "Belly-five!" he shouts. This time Tess is ready for him; as Cole jumps with his belly towards her, Tess meets him with her stomach out.

"Another round?" Matt asks.

Cole rubs his abdomen. "I say new teams." He looks at me playfully.

I can't help but notice the look on Matt's face at Cole's suggestion. I don't like the idea of Tess climbing on top of Matt's back either.

Even Tess is quiet.

It shouldn't be a big deal. It's not like there's anything wrong with his idea.

"Come on!" Cole shouts. "Switch partners."

All three of us are standing still in the lake. I'm glad I'm not the only one uncomfortable.

Cole laughs again and turns to Matt. "On my back! We're going to destroy the girls."

Matt laughs, breaking the tension. Cole goes onto all

fours in the water, keeping his head up, while Matt climbs on his back and onto his shoulders. As Cole stands, he almost loses his balance.

"Whoa!" he shouts. "A lot heavier than you seem."

"Shut up!" Matt quips. "We're going to lose before we even start. Buck up!"

Tess and I agree that she should be the one on my back since she's thinner and lighter weight. A basic strategy that the men seem to have not thought out. Cole shouts like a gorilla as he attempts to come closer to us, nearly falling in the water as he does.

Tess laughs and puts her hands up as she makes contact with Matt. As Matt tries to push her, Tess moves to the side and with all her might shoves Matt, causing him to lose balance. To aid her, I splash water in Cole's eyes. He screams and the two fall into the water.

"The women are undefeated!" I shout. As the men come up from the water, they both playfully give us sour faces.

"You're right, Matt," Cole says. "Cheating is wrong. I see that now that I've watched your fiancée flagrantly violate the rules of chicken fighting."

After the men admit defeat, the four of us relax on the beach on our chairs, drinking. The sun beats down on us. I take in the smells of the beach and the blue water.

Life feels good. Especially now that I've rediscovered my lost ability to write words.

I sit on the first chair, with Cole beside me, then Tess and Matt. The four of us laugh as we talk about random things.

Cole sits up. He looks over at me. Even with his sunglasses on, I can see his eyes wander on my body. I try not to notice his stare and move in the chair, grabbing the towel from behind me and using it as a blanket.

"Getting cold," I say.

Cole nods. "Well, I need more beer. Do you need another drink?" I shake my head. Matt says he wants another beer while Tess says she is fine. Cole comes back soon with two beers, stumbling on the beach as he does. He laughs as he nearly falls.

I wonder how many drinks he's had. Matt's giggling just as much as him. Cole hands him a beer and sits back down on the beach chair beside me.

"I have to ask," he says looking at me, "How do you come up with this stuff?"

I laugh. "You mean my stories?"

Cole looks at Tess. "I've been reading her book and man, it's just nuts. The serial killer main character girl. She's straight up murdering people in the most messed-up ways possible. I'm only like a dozen or so chapters in and she's killed someone by throwing a pot of boiling sugar at them." He turns to me and smiles. "I mean, how do you come up with that stuff?"

I laugh. "Us mystery writers are all messed-up people." I point my finger at him. "So don't mess with us."

Matt laughs. "One time I had to use her laptop to search for something. I discovered her browser history as I typed in Google. How to get away with murder. Best place to hide a body... If something ever happens to me, please just assume Sidney had something to do with it."

I laugh. "I'm most definitely flagged by the police at this point."

Cole nods his head. "As you should be. I'll have to pick your brain though."

"What do you mean?"

Cole opens his beer bottle and flicks the cap into the

water. "I told you I want to be a writer."

"Here we go again," Tess says playfully.

Cole quickly looks at her and she turns over in her beach chair. "I mean it," he says, looking back at me. "I've got some ideas outlined. I'm just trying to make it all connect and it's just… not. I think I've spent years trying to figure out how to make this story work."

"What genre is it?" I ask, interested in what he says.

"Well, yours," he says with a smile. "Thrillers. Dark ones. I love your story from what I've read so far. I can see why you're so popular. You seriously have a natural skill."

I smile. "I have you to thank, I suppose. You're the one who started my love for reading. I guess I should give credit."

Cole grins. "You can pay me back by helping me with my novel."

"Anytime," I say. I sit up in my beach chair, the towel falling to my abdomen.

Matt sits up in his chair and takes a sip of his beer. "Sidney's writing again," he says with a smile. "She took a bit of a long break."

"Writer's block?" Tess asks.

I don't feel it was, but I don't want to get into that with them. "I guess, yeah."

"What's it about?" Cole asks.

"Well," I say, with a laugh. "Kind of about this place." I gesture at the lake and the house. "I think a secluded lake house is a great setting."

"What about your characters?" Cole says. Tess sits up in her chair now, waiting for my answer.

"Uh," I say, trying to find the right words. "It's about a couple who're at a lake house. The girlfriend suspects that her fiancé is up to something. There's going to be a lot of misunderstandings and clues that support her and why she feels so strongly that something is wrong. There will also be events that make her second-guess herself. Eventually, she turns out to be right."

"The boyfriend is the bad guy?" Cole says with a smile.

I nod my head slowly. "That's right. It's going to be a survival thriller."

"What's the character's name?" Cole asks. He turns to Tess. "I always wondered how authors come up with them."

"I don't have them yet," I admit, while not telling them the full truth.

"Oh," Cole says. "You've been writing this book for a while and don't have names for your characters?"

I smile and look out over the lake, wishing I could get out of this conversation, but I don't see a way. "I sort of give them names for now, until I come up with something better."

"So what are you temporarily calling them?" Cole asks.

I squirm in my chair, wondering what to say. I'm a terrible liar. "Well, this is just for now, but I'm calling them Tess and Cole."

Tess looks at me and Cole smiles.

"Wait a minute," he says. "I'm the villain in your story?" His grin gets larger. "Awesome. It makes me feel terrible. And you have my permission to kill me off. Make it one of your crazy, messed-up ways like in the story I'm reading."

"You're writing about me?" Tess says, confused. "Is it bad? Why would you do that?"

I shake my head. "No, no. It's just for inspirational

purposes. I can't think of anything and sometimes I use the names of people I know until I do."

"She used my name in some of her books before," Matt chimes in. "I was the husband in one of her rough manuscripts. The husband who died tragically, by the way." He lowers his sunglasses and smirks at me.

I shake my head. "It's not meant to be an insult to either of you." When Tess doesn't answer, I shake my head. "Sorry. I didn't mean to hurt your feelings."

"We're fine," Cole says. "Honored, really. I get to be a villain." He burps loudly. "Make me an awesome one."

CHAPTER 21

Cole makes a seafood boil on the beach for dinner. It's amazing! Lobster, shrimp, potatoes, salted and boiled in butter over a fire. I'm stuffed after.
I'm surprised he was capable of cooking dinner near a fire without falling into it. All four of us had too much to drink. It wasn't just Cole and Matt giggling like long lost brothers; Tess and I were too.
As the sun sets, we decide to move our shenanigans to a campfire. The four of us drink some more and melt marshmallows for smores. Cole mocks Tess by smudging some marshmallow on her nose but remedies it by licking the gooeyness off. Matt and I holler and cheer them on.
For a moment, Matt looks at me and I catch his glance. I can tell he wants to kiss me, and for a change, he acts on it. He gets off his chair and grabs me, kissing me hard. This time Cole and Tess cheer us on.
I'm not one for public affection, especially one so bold, but in the moment, I love it.
"Congrats again on your new story," Tess says to me.
Cole is melting a marshmallow on his skewer. He shoves it in the fire while taking a long drink of his beer. "Cheers! To Sidney's new book and to me as her main character!"
The four of us clink our drinks together. I thank them all.

As much fun as I'm having, I have to admit I'm not fully in the moment. Whenever I'm knee deep in a new story, my mind wanders all the time as to what the characters in my book are doing.

I suppose it's okay to let my thoughts run free, especially since I'm being inspired by the real Cole and Tess. Every so often though, I'll look up at the lake house at the office window and feel the urge to write something. Maybe I'll sneak in some words tonight. I'm not sure how. In my current state, I don't feel anything I write would be usable when I look at it the next day.

"So, what do you do, Tess?" Matt asks. "I don't think I asked before."

"Well, I'm sort of figuring things out," Tess says, brushing her hair back behind her shoulder and taking a sip of her beer.

"That means she has no clue." Cole laughs. Tess rolls her eyes. "What? You don't," he says in his defence.

"I don't know," Tess says. "I feel so envious of people like you, Sidney." She turns to me with a thin smile. "I mean, you know what you want to do, and look at you now. You're a writer and doing great."

I nod. "Well, that's true, but it took a lot to get here. Don't think it happens overnight. You just have to figure out what you enjoy doing and go for it. Do you have anything that interests you?"

Cole laughs again. "Spending your parents' money." This time I kick him in the lower leg. I know Tess is scared to do it, but I can't help it.

"Stop it, Cole," I tell him. "You're being a drunk."

"Hey! No hitting." Cole throws some of his marshmallow towards me but misses on purpose. "Tess doesn't have to worry like us; her parents are loaded." He gestures toward the house. "Look at this place. How many acres is it? It's all her parents'. Her father's, specifically. If I were you, Tess, I wouldn't care. You could be a professional knitter and be perfectly fine for the rest of your life."

Tess scoffs. "I want something for myself, Cole."

Cole shakes his head. "Your parents will take care of you. You're their only child. Who do you think inherits all of this when the time comes? This is all yours. The money your dad has is yours. You don't have to worry. Once you inherit it all, you can be an investor or own some properties. I can help you."

Tess takes a long drink of her beer but doesn't answer.

"Sign me up for that life," Matt jokes.

"Right?" Cole laughs. When he sees that Tess is not happily joining the conversation, he sighs. "I'm not being rude. I'm just telling you how it is. You don't have to worry. People like me have to worry."

Tess looks at him sternly. "Do you really have to worry, Doctor Cole?" she says with a funny tone.

Cole points a finger at her. "You stop that now."

Tess quickly gets up from her chair and hurries down the beach.

"Tess!" I call out to her, but she doesn't stop. I watch as her body disappears past the glow of the fire, into the night.

"Tess!" Cole shouts in a sterner voice. "Come on. Come back." He stands up now. He finishes his beer before tossing the bottle into the flames. "I guess the princess is mad at the prince. I have to court her majesty now." He walks into the dark, following Tess slowly, stumbling along the way.

I look at Matt who seems just as put off as me. "Do they always fight like this?" he asks. I shrug. "Tess says they do. She tells me it's this vicious cycle of fighting, making up and more fighting." "Gosh," Matt says, taking a sip of his beer. "I'm glad we're not like that." He smiles at me. "I love you."

"I love you too," I say back without hesitation. We've had a rocky road for some time, but being here at the lake house, it feels like everything is changing. It's almost like I'm rediscovering why I love Matt, and also my love for writing.

"Should we go find them?" he asks. He finishes his beer and throws it into the fire like Cole. I give him a look to let him know I'm not impressed, and he apologizes.

"I'm sure it's better if we don't get involved," I answer.

Matt nods. "In your story, is this the part where Cole tries to kill her?" He laughs, but I don't. Instead, my imagination is already running away with ideas of what the couple are doing.

CHAPTER 22

I lay my head on Matt's chest as we sit in silence, enjoying the fire.

"They've been a while," Matt says. "I was just joking before, but maybe we should check on them."

I finish my bottle and take a deep breath. "I'm sure they're fine."

While Matt may be enjoying the fire and my warmth, I've been somewhere else in my mind. I can't stop thinking about the characters of Cole and Tess in the book I'm writing. What would happen at this point if Cole showed his true colors? How would Tess survive? I've only written a few thousand words. I can't make such a big reveal so early, or can I?

I imagine a scene in my head of Cole using his charms to disarm Tess's character into thinking she's safe. Getting her vulnerable to the point where she doesn't see her own demise is around the corner.

I look out at the lake house, and the office upstairs. I need to write down my thoughts. When I write a story, I always have something to jot notes on in case something pops into my head. If I can get to the office, I can quickly make some bullet points. I know from experience that on the times I didn't make notes when I had ideas for scenes, I'd completely forgotten how I imagined them later on.

"I'm proud of you, by the way," Matt says, wrapping

his arm around me. He kisses the side of my head. "I know how hard it's been for you to write, and look at what you've done."

"Thanks," I say looking into the fire.

"Maybe for the rest of our time here, you should take a rest from writing, though. You know, enjoy your time like this. This is our vacation after all." He kisses the side of my head again.

I take a deep breath. I don't want to fight with him again. I haven't written like this in forever and he wants me to stop? I can't. I worry if I do, I'll go back to how I use to be. I'm inspired out here, and I need to use it.

"You had fun today, right?" I ask.

He nods his head. "Loved it."

"Well, I wrote a lot today, and we had a great time. Sometimes we can do both."

He sighs. "Okay. That's true."

"I'll try not to write as much and take away from our days here before we leave. When we get back home, though, I'll catch up. I have a lot to make up for to hit the deadline the publisher gave me. I think I can talk to Vanessa and tell her what I'm doing. It's not what we talked about, but I think she'll love what I have so far." I sigh, thinking about my limited cell service. "I'll have to email her though."

Matt looks at me. "Are you sure about that? What if you see something that upsets you?"

I don't answer him. I'm worried as well. I imagine the flood of email IWriteAlone may have sent me since I last checked my emails. If they have, I won't even look at them. I'll delete anything immediately.

"I can check your emails for you," Matt offers. "I just don't want you to get upset, love."

"I know," I say as I snuggle into his large chest. I get those thoughts out of my mind and think of my story again.

I don't tell Matt that nearly the entire time we've been relaxing together my head's been somewhere else. He hates it when I do this. He'd always tell me that I'm not in the moment. It's true. I'm not. It's hard for me, though. It's like living in two realities at once. One's a fictional one and one is really happening.

I also don't tell him that now that I'm not giving back my advance, I'll likely have to start the book signing tour again. As he said, that will be a conversation for after we leave.

The scene of Cole and Tess is still playing out in my mind though. I look over at the lake house again. I can't tell Matt that I need to make some notes for the book. I know it'll upset him.

I finish my beer. "I'm going to grab another drink. Do you want anything?"

"I'm good."

I stand up from the chair, but so does Matt. "No, it's okay," I say. "Enjoy the fire."

Matt smiles and sits down in his chair again.

I walk towards the lake house. Once I'm inside, I'll quickly grab a notepad or a piece of paper from the office and make my notes for the scene that is still running in my mind.

I hurry towards the house once I feel I'm out of sight of Matt. As I near the patio doors, I hear a muffled scream. It stops me in my tracks, and I look around the dark patio and out onto the beach. All I see is Matt sitting by the fire.

Then I hear a shriek. It's definitely a woman.

"Tess?" I say into the darkness.

Then I see a shadowy figure on the beach. I walk closer towards the muffled sounds until I can see a silhouette of a woman. She's arching her head and upper back against a large tree. A leg is raised and pressed against another tree beside her. Below her is another shadowy figure of a man.

Nestled between Tess's thighs, I see the head of Cole moving rapidly. It takes a moment in my drunken stupor to realize what I'm witnessing. The muffled sounds of pleasure from Tess confirm it.

Tess did say she enjoyed making up after fighting with Cole. I guess I know why. I feel frozen as I see the shadows continue. Finally, I snap out of it, take a step backwards, and quickly make my way back to the fire.

"Hey," Matt says as I get closer. "Did you forget your drink?" He laughs.

I give him a thin smile. "Changed my mind."

CHAPTER 23

Tess and Cole arrive at the campfire again. Tess has a grin on her face wider than anything I've ever seen. Cole has his usual smirk.

"There you two are," Matt jokes. "I was getting worried and about to send a search party for you." Cole and Tess laugh.

Matt yawns as he stands up. "I'm beat, guys. I'm heading to bed."

"I'll come too," I say.

"I know what you two are going to do," Cole jokes, pointing at us.

"Cole!" Tess says playfully. "Stop it."

Matt laughs. "Goodnight, guys." He grabs my hand as we walk towards the house. We're quiet as we head up the stairs.

Once we are in the guest bedroom, Matt closes the door behind him. He makes a face when he looks at it. "No locks. Perfect." He comes up to me and kisses me passionately. As his kisses move from my lips to my neckline, all I can think about is the story in my head.

I think about Cole's character. How he uses his sexuality to dominate Tess. Or is it the other way around?

If only I can start writing the scene. I know I can make it perfect right now. I have the tone in my head. It's like a reel of a movie that I can't pause. If I don't write it now, the show will be over."

"Let's not," I whisper to Matt.

"What?" he says as he kisses my shoulder.

"I don't know. It's not our house. It feels weird. I think I drank too much too."

Matt scoffs and sits on the bed. "I thought we had a good time today."

I sit beside him. "We did. So much fun. I'm just tired."

Matt kisses me, the passion he had a few moments ago now gone and a new expression of defeat on his face.

"Okay." We kiss again after we change into our nightwear and are in the sheets.

It doesn't take long for me to hear his deep breathing as he falls asleep. My plan is working perfectly. Maybe another ten minutes or so, and I can go to the office and do what I have to do.

I need to get the scene out of my head and onto a page.

Somehow, patiently waiting for Matt to fully fall asleep, I begin to get tired myself. I did have too much today.

Matt moves to his side, and I realize he's not as tired as I thought. I close my eyes and wait until I fall asleep myself.

When I hear a creak, my eyes open. I hear it again, louder. I blink a few times, expecting to see Matt out of the bed. He must have left for the bathroom, but when I turn to my side, he's sleeping peacefully.

I don't hear any footsteps down the hallway either. The bedroom door is shut.

Was I dreaming?

I look at Matt and confirm that he's asleep. My fiancé

is certainly in dreamland.

    I slip out of bed and sneak into the office, making the minimum number of squeaks on the floorboards as I can. When I look outside the office window, I see a smoldering fire where we were tonight. I noticed that Tess and Cole's bedroom door was shut when I passed. They must be asleep as well.

    I take in a deep breath and smile. There's something about knowing you have a whole house to yourself that helps the creativity break through. No one can interrupt me. No one can stop the movie in my head from playing. I can put all my attention into my story.

    I don't tend to skip scenes when I'm writing. I like to write a book from the beginning to end and not jump around, but after what I saw tonight, I'm moved to write a bit of a spicy scene with my characters. I also don't tend to write sexual scenes as well, but tonight I feel different.

    I log into the guest profile and anxiously wait to start writing as the slow computer starts up. While I wait, I play the events in my head. A spicy scene with Cole and Tess. Something to show how connected they are but also a hint that something may be wrong.

    I had it perfect in my head at the campfire but after waiting to write it for so long and falling asleep, with no notes, I feel lost already. I'm almost tempted to go back to sleep as the words aren't coming to me, but I try and replay the scene.

    Instead, all I see is Cole, doing what he did to Tess, only in my mind, it's me. I breathe deep and try to get my head back into the actual story.

    A creak of the office door startles me. It slowly opens, but nobody is there. I wait for someone to enter the room, but all I see is the dark hallway.

"Hello?" I call out. I put a hand to my chest when no one answers me.

The door continues to slowly creak open until it stops. I can see into the dark hallway but don't hear anyone or see anything.

"Hello?" I say again.

A hand wraps around the doorframe and waves at me. A moment later, Cole enters the room, giggling to himself.

I finally catch my breath. "What are you doing?"

"I've come to finish you off," he says, twiddling his fingers, making a ghost sound. "I'm working on my evilness... You're up late. Writing?"

I nod my head. "Trying. The scene managed to escape me, though."

"I can help," Cole says. "It will be just like the old days. I can tutor you. Teach you." He purses his lips as he waits for my reply.

"Uh, well, it's okay. I'm fine. I think I might just go back to sleep."

Cole shakes his head. "Disappointing." He looks out into the hallway. "Tess is asleep. Matt too?"

I nod my head. "Yeah, I think we all had too much to drink."

He locks eyes with me for a moment before looking away. "You remember the first kiss we had?" I take my hands off the keyboard. "I do," he continues. "It was at your house. I was supposed to be tutoring you. We were going over your book report for—"

"*The Catcher in the Rye*," I say.

He smiles. "That's right. The report you had was complete garbage too."

"It wasn't that bad."

He nods his head. "No insights whatsoever. It was just a regurgitation of the story. I knew you could do better, and you did, with my help."

I take a deep breath. There's something about the way he's looking at me that has me scared. Not about what he might try but what I might let happen.

Cole steps closer to me. "After our kiss, we went to the local fair they had going, remember? We took a bunch of photos at that booth they had. It sounds weird, but I kept those photos. Still have them."

I stand up from the desk and clear my throat. "I should go back to sleep. Have a good night, Cole."

Before I leave, he grabs my wrist, hard. "Tell me," he says, giving me a devilish stare, "would you be as good of a writer if it wasn't for me?"

I anxiously laugh, wondering when he'll let go. "I don't know. I probably would have failed English."

He finally releases my arm. "And yet, no appreciation. Nothing about me."

"What?"

"I looked it up, wondering if you'd given me credit somewhere. An interview or something. Anything. I even checked your books to see if you dedicated anything to me for what I did for you."

I wait a moment, thinking he must be joking. I know I'll see that stupid smirk on his face soon. Instead, he looks at me intensely.

"I never make dedications in my books," I say, confused by the change in his mood. "It feels weird to write about murdering husbands and cheaters and dedicate it to a loved one, or anyone for that matter."

He nods. "Well, maybe you'll dedicate your next story to me. You better." He locks eyes with me. "I mean, it is only right. The story is about me, and this house. This time I should get credit for something I've done."

He continues to stare me down. His eyes look so angry. I don't understand how I've upset him though.

Before I can say another word, Cole brushes past me and leaves the office. I hear his footsteps as he walks down the hall to his bedroom.

CHAPTER 24

It takes me a few moments to collect myself after Cole interrupted my writing session.

What exactly was his intention? At first, I was worried he would try to make a move on me, then, for a brief moment, he scared me.

I'm not entirely sure how to feel, but I'm left alone now, completely uncomfortable.

I look at the computer, and part of me, the creative trooper side of my personality, wants to sit down and use it to write a hell of a scene. The other side of me wants to leave and go back to the guest room with Matt.

An inner voice thinks about leaving. Not just this office but this house. We're supposed to stay another night, but I wonder if we should after that encounter with Cole.

I truly had a great time today, up until a few moments ago. The more I stay here, the more I worry about myself. Cole is becoming more and more tempting to me, but on the other hand, more volatile.

He's just drunk, I tell myself. And while that may be true, I don't want to be around it. We only have another night here.

Then again, there's a part of me that's been reborn at this lake house. I've written so much in one night, I wonder how much more I would get done if I stayed more than a night.

Wouldn't it be worth changing my flight and staying longer if it meant writing another ten thousand words? How much would that be worth? Could be a lot if the book does well.

I'm inspired here. Will I find the same inspiration at our place in Chestermere? Or will I go back to my old ways? Scared of my own shadow. Scared to write a single word.

I hear the floorboards creak and quickly make up my mind. No more writing tonight. I save my document before logging off the computer.

Too late. I hear a door open and footsteps coming towards the office. I'm worried what Cole will do when he approaches me. Will he reminisce about our romance from our youth some more? Will he make a move on me? Or will he act however he was before he left?

It's all so confusing. I don't even know what I want to happen. Part of me wants him to come back to the office. Play out the scene I have in my mind in real life. It's just a fantasy. It's okay to fantasize, isn't it?

What if it went beyond just thoughts?

Matt cheated on me. Is this how I get back at him?

The creaking stops right outside the office. I hold my breath, waiting for Cole to come into the room. Instead, Tess knocks on the door and gives me a thin smile.

"Hey," she says.

"Hi."

"Are you still writing?" she asks.

I shake my head. "All done. I'm tired. I think I'll get some rest, maybe try again tomorrow."

She nods and rubs the side of the door. "Are you having fun here? With Cole and me?"

I nod too. "Today was great. It was just what Matt and I needed."

She grins. "Good." She looks out into the hallway towards her room and back at me. "Are you sure you're tired? You want to have some more drinks?"

"I don't usually drink like I did today. I know I'll pay for it tomorrow. I think I'm done tonight."

"Okay," she says. She meets my eyes and looks away. "I'm going to go back to my bed with Cole."

I look around the room. "Well, okay. Um, have a good night."

She nods. "Do you want to join us?"

"Join you?" I repeat.

She meets my eyes and smiles. "Cole wanted me to ask."

I gaze down at the floor, my mouth gaping wide. I can only imagine what I look like in response.

"Sorry," Tess says, waving her hand. "Forget it." Tess lowers her head. "Goodnight." She hurries out of the room, and I hear her walking down the hall.

I cover my head, hiding my face, hoping that I misunderstood what Tess was asking.

No more writing tonight. I feel the urge to scurry back to the guest room and hide under the covers with Matt.

Matt. Should I even tell him about tonight? I need to sleep. I let out a single laugh over the silliness of it all.

As I leave the office, Tess and Cole's bedroom door is wide open. A dim light enters the hallway, illuminating the guest room.

For a brief moment, I wonder what it would be like to enter their room. What would happen if I did? A flash of the silhouettes in the dark of Cole and Tess on the beach hits me. I breathe in deep and stare at the shadow the light from their room is casting on the door where Matt's sleeping.

I glance back at Cole's bedroom, only this time he's standing in the doorway. He's shirtless in his tight Calvin Klein boxer briefs, staring at me intensely.

I quickly make my decision and open the guest bedroom door, then close it gently behind me. I hear a loud thud of Cole closing his door.

I look over at Matt in the bed. The sound of the door crashing shut made him turn over but he's still fast asleep. I'm not sure if I'm scared or excited, but I try to lock the door. Is it because I want no one to enter the room, or I'm scared I'll try to leave to go to theirs?

I sigh when I realize there's no lock on the door. I breathe in deep as I slowly get into the covers. I lay in bed, staring at the ceiling and turning over. Matt is breathing deeply, on the verge of snoring. For a moment, his eyes flutter open and stare at me. Our gazes meet for a brief moment before he yawns and turns to the other side.

CHAPTER 24

It takes me a few moments to collect myself after Cole interrupted my writing session.

What exactly was his intention? At first, I was worried he would try to make a move on me, then, for a brief moment, he scared me.

I'm not entirely sure how to feel, but I'm left alone now, completely uncomfortable.

I look at the computer, and part of me, the creative trooper side of my personality, wants to sit down and use it to write a hell of a scene. The other side of me wants to leave and go back to the guest room with Matt.

An inner voice thinks about leaving. Not just this office but this house. We're supposed to stay another night, but I wonder if we should after that encounter with Cole.

I truly had a great time today, up until a few moments ago. The more I stay here, the more I worry about myself. Cole is becoming more and more tempting to me, but on the other hand, more volatile.

He's just drunk, I tell myself. And while that may be true, I don't want to be around it. We only have another night here.

Then again, there's a part of me that's been reborn at this lake house. I've written so much in one night, I wonder how much more I would get done if I stayed more than a night.

Wouldn't it be worth changing my flight and staying longer if it meant writing another ten thousand words? How much would that be worth? Could be a lot if the book does well.

I'm inspired here. Will I find the same inspiration at our place in Chestermere? Or will I go back to my old ways? Scared of my own shadow. Scared to write a single word.

I hear the floorboards creak and quickly make up my mind. No more writing tonight. I save my document before logging off the computer.

Too late. I hear a door open and footsteps coming towards the office. I'm worried what Cole will do when he approaches me. Will he reminisce about our romance from our youth some more? Will he make a move on me? Or will he act however he was before he left?

It's all so confusing. I don't even know what I want to happen. Part of me wants him to come back to the office. Play out the scene I have in my mind in real life. It's just a fantasy. It's okay to fantasize, isn't it?

What if it went beyond just thoughts?

Matt cheated on me. Is this how I get back at him?

The creaking stops right outside the office. I hold my breath, waiting for Cole to come into the room. Instead, Tess knocks on the door and gives me a thin smile.

"Hey," she says.

"Hi."

"Are you still writing?" she asks.

I shake my head. "All done. I'm tired. I think I'll get some rest, maybe try again tomorrow."

She nods and rubs the side of the door. "Are you having fun here? With Cole and me?"

CHAPTER 25

I toss and turn through the night, finding it difficult to sleep. My mind won't stop racing.

What would it have been like had I accepted Tess's offer? What would Cole have done had I gone into his bedroom instead of my own? While part of me felt the excitement of the idea, the other side of me knew it would destroy Matt. How could I do that to a man I love? To a man I plan to marry?

I was crushed after Matt kissed another woman. I'm still not over it. In no way would going into Cole's room have made things better between us.

I know that.

When I wake up, Matt is not in bed. I stretch out my arms as the strong morning light shines through the window. I wonder how long I've been sleeping for.

I turn my head and notice the bedroom door is wide open. Why does Matt do that? Yesterday morning he left the door open. Today he's done the same. A thought hits me.

Did Cole watch me as I slept? The idea makes me uneasy.

What's the opposite of wearing out a welcome? I think I'm ready to leave the lake house. We're supposed to have another night here, but I don't think I can handle that anymore. Not after what happened last night.

I need to talk to Matt. He needs to agree that it's time to leave. The question I'm wondering is how much to tell him? Should I say everything that happened last night? The odd behaviour. The invitation to their bedroom.

Certainly, Matt would be upset. No matter how much fun we had yesterday during the day, what happened at night puts a sour taste in my mouth.

I get out of bed, close the door and quickly change. Part of me is nervous the door will open again, and Cole will be there while I undress.

I open the bedroom door and look up and down the hallway. This morning, I don't hear Cole and Matt laughing hysterically downstairs. It's oddly quiet, but maybe it's the tension in my own mind.

I look at the office door and quickly go inside, closing it behind me. Thankfully this room has a lock and I use it, ensuring I won't have any unwanted guests this time.

I go to the computer and log on.

I need to make things right with my publisher. I have a good start to a novel and can expand on the story when I get home, but I need to talk to Vanessa. I'm sure I can turn things around. Our last meeting was terrible, but I hope she'll be receptive to talking again.

I'm not able to call her though. There's no cell service out here. There's only one way to get a hold of her. Email. I haven't been logged into mine for a very long time. Last time I was in tears as I continuously read the multiple emails IWriteAlone sent me. I still remember Matt begging me, as I cried into his shoulder, to delete my account.

I didn't delete it but stopped using it completely. Until today.

I open a browser and it takes forever. Despite being a "famous author" I still mostly use a Gmail account for my communications. I enter my account name and password and hit enter. The page turns white and thinks about my request, taking forever to access my email.

Part of me wonders if I'll even be able to. If I haven't used this account in over a year, will I be able to still use it?

The screen stays white while the computer thinks about my request. I'm about to give up on the idea when my account finally opens.

I smile as I immediately start an email to Vanessa. I open my Word document and fix a few things before attaching it to the email. First, I write a sincere apology to her for how I was at the meeting a few days ago. I tell her a little about my story and the directions I'm thinking of taking it. I tell her a little about my characters, Cole and Tess as well. I let her know that I believe I can finish the story on time to meet the publisher's deadline. I explain how motivated I am and finish the email with another apology.

Before I can hit send, someone knocks gently on the door.

"Hello?" I call out. I don't want to open the door. I would rather not. I'd be fine with not talking to Cole again. It hits me that he wants to drive us to the airport and the idea of being in a car with him and Matt frightens me.

The knock continues.

I clear my throat and walk up to it. "Who is it?"

"It's me, Tess," she says in a quiet voice.

"Oh, hey," I say through the door. "I'm just doing some work. Is it okay to do that in the office?"

"Can we talk?" she asks.

"Uh, well, I'm almost done."

"Please." I can hear her sniffle.

I breathe in deep as I unlock the door and open it slowly. Tess stands in the hallway, her eyes watery and hands in her jean pockets.

"Hey," she says softly.

"Are you okay?" I ask.

She nods. "I'm just so embarrassed. Last night. I was drunk. I don't know what I was thinking... Cole talked me into doing something stupid. I'm just so sorry about it all."

I nod my head. "I get it, but I'm okay. I'm just... with Matt, so it was weird for me."

She nods back. "Of course. It was stupid. I should have told Cole no, but he had this weird attitude last night."

I think about how Cole was with me before he left the office. He scared me and excited me all at once.

"It's okay," I tell her. "Really. I was put off, but I appreciate you talking to me today about it."

She lets out a sigh. "I can only imagine what you think of me now."

I smile. "Well, I went off the rails yesterday a little bit. So I guess it's even."

She smiles. "Okay. I'll let you get back to your work."

"Thanks," I say. "And thanks for letting me use your office. I really am grateful that I came here this weekend. The story is really coming together."

"Happy to hear," Tess says. She takes a few steps backwards before leaving down the hallway towards the stairs.

I close the door slowly and, once it's shut, lock it

quickly. Sitting in the office chair, I finish rereading my email to Vanessa. Satisfied with my apology to her, I lean back in the chair and hover the mouse over the send button.

If the email goes to her, that's it. I'm committed. I have to finish my story. No more messing around. I only have a few months to complete it. Even if my writing speed is half of what I've had since being at the lake house, I'll finish the book well before the deadline.

That is if Vanessa agrees to continue working with me.

I've been through a lot, and she knows it. Vanessa can be unsympathetic at times, but she does have an understanding for my situation. When the emails from the stalker first started, we would talk for over an hour on the phone about my concerns. Vanessa had a very calming effect on me back then.

But that didn't matter.

If she's still willing to offer therapy, I should accept it.

I can still be the author I want to be. I just have to get over everything that happened. Just like my character Tess in my story, I need to face my fears.

I hit send and my email quickly vanishes. I wonder how Vanessa will react when she sees it.

I smile as I notice how many unopened emails I have in my account. I wonder how many were important business-related ones and how many were from marketing people or author services bothering me for business.

How many were from fans.

As I look at the first email, I get my answer. My smile quickly vanishes as I read who sent it. The subject line reads, "I'm still your biggest fan." IWriteAlone has sent a new email.

I click on it and attached is an image of the grocery store that we went to yesterday. Below it, IWriteAlone wrote, "See you around."

CHAPTER 26

I head down the stairs, trying to keep myself composed. Just as Tess was moments ago, I'm on the verge of breaking down in tears. I nearly trip over my feet on one step and only stop myself from falling by grabbing onto the handrail.

I take several deep breaths, trying to calm my nerves, but I know it's hopeless. I let go of the handrail and can feel my hand shaking uncontrollably.

I could curl up in a ball and cry on the stairway if it wasn't for me wanting to find Matt. He wasn't in bed. He's likely up somewhere with Cole. I'm sure Cole's making another breakfast with a stupid face on it.

As I get to the bottom of the stairs safely, I see Tess and Cole sitting at the dining table together, speaking quietly. As I walk up to them, Cole takes a sip of his coffee. Tess gives me a thin smile, but Cole ignores my presence completely.

"Where's Matt?" I ask.

"Good morning to you as well," Cole says, blowing into his mug and taking another sip.

"Where is he?" I repeat frantically.

He turns to me, confused. "I don't know. Sleeping?"

"He's not in bed," I say. "Where did he go?"

Cole laughs. "I'm not sure. Relax. You can be a lot, you know that?"

"Cole," Tess says quietly.

"Don't give me that attitude," he says to her. "She's the one freaking out." Tess gives him a look and suddenly his features soften as he looks at me again. "Sorry. A little hungover from last night. I'm being a moody dude. Want breakfast?" He gestures to his coffee mug. "A morning beverage?"

I take a step back. "I need to find Matt. You haven't seen him?"

"Nope," Cole says. Tess just stares at me quietly.

"Where could he have gone?" I say frantically. "We're in the middle of nowhere."

"An epic game of hide and seek, I guess," Cole says, laughing as he takes a sip.

I take a deep breath. "I need to find him. I have to talk to him."

"Alright, relax," Cole says, taking another sip. "I'm sure he's somewhere." He smiles at Tess.

There's something about his reaction that strikes me. I'm not sure if it's my nerves, but everything in my body is yelling at me that something is wrong. Very wrong.

I woke up to an email from IWriteAlone and now I can't find Matt. He's not in the house. Where could he have gone?

I open the patio door and look out towards the beach. I don't see him. I don't see anyone. There aren't even boats on the lake this morning. I look towards the firepit area but all I see are burnt logs and a few beer bottles scattered around.

Cole leans against the doorframe, taking another sip of his coffee. He spills some of it on his red shirt and grimaces, wiping it with his hand. "You seem a little off today, Sidney." He smiles at me as he takes another sip. His blue eyes stare me down as a smirk stays on his face. He's enjoying this. Me being scared is entertaining him.

I look out towards the beach and the lake, hoping, praying to see him. "Matt!" I shout. I look back and Cole's smirk turns into a grin. I turn from him. "Matt! Where are you!"

CHAPTER 27

"Matt!" I yell again.

"Matthew!" Cole yells, mocking me.

I turn to him, my eyes full of anger and confusion. "Where is he?" I yell.

"How am I supposed to know?" he says between laughs. "Man, I'm too hung over for this. I thought you got your crazies out yesterday."

"Cole!" Tess shouts behind him.

He shakes his head and drinks his coffee. "It's ridiculous, Tess."

"Help her find him," Tess says. "She's scared."

"Why is she so scared? What did we do?"

My hands are at my side and are trembling uncontrollably. Cole watches me, amused.

"IWriteAlone," I say again.

Cole raises his eyebrows. "Here we go. I'm the stalker again. The bad guy." He smiles. "Fine." He gives Tess his coffee mug. "Let's go find your *dear* fiancé."

He takes a step towards me, and I point at him. "Stop. Just leave me alone. I don't know what games you're playing with me, but I'm done with them."

Tess walks in front of him. "Sidney. What—"

"Both of you stop," I say. I start to head towards the beach, looking back frequently as I do. Both Cole and Tess watch me as I go.

I turn through some bushes but stay on the beach. Thankfully, the couple are out of sight, and I hurry my pace.

"Matt!" I yell again.

Where is he?

The other night at the fire, Matt joked that Cole had done something terrible to Tess. This morning, I woke up and found an email from IWriteAlone. Has something happened to Matt?

I want to go home. I want to leave here.

I never want to see Cole or Tess ever again.

"Matt!" I can feel my heart pulsing as I continue down the beach. I stop and look back where I started, hoping to see him. Should I try heading down the other side of the beach instead? He could be anywhere.

What if something happened to him? I joked that this area was perfect to hide a body. It's how my imagination works but what if it's no longer just thoughts?

I imagine walking down the beach and finding him. Waves crashing against his corpse as I confirm for myself that Matt is dead. Why does my imagination jump to the worst situations that could happen?

"Where are you?" I shout. I look back down the beach and this time see Cole standing and watching me.

The two of us continue to stare at each other. I realize I'm holding my breath and can feel myself getting dizzy with fear. Cole starts walking towards me. I turn and run into the thick trees beyond the beach.

I don't look back. I don't yell for my fiancé. Now I'm just running. As I do, I trip over a rock and fall forward. I stretch out my arms to catch my fall and feel a twinge in my right arm. I scream out in pain. I look back toward the path I took into the woods.

Cole would have heard me. It won't take long for him to catch up. I stand up quickly and realize I banged my right knee as well. I continue through the woods as fast as possible, my knee aching with pain.

Suddenly I see movement behind me through some trees. I catch a man quickly walking. I see a red shirt.

"Leave me alone!" I shout at Cole.

I watch in terror as the bushes begin to move and I can see him walking towards me. I let out a breath when I realize who it is.

"Sidney?" Matt whips his hand past a thick bush as he walks past it. "Who are you screaming at?" He looks at my bruised arm and scrape on my knee. "What happened?"

I run up to him and hug him. Tears are freely falling from my eyes; I can't believe I've found him.

I let go of him and shake his sides. "Where the hell were you?"

He looks at me, confused. "I went for a hike."

"A hike?" I repeat.

"Everyone was still sleeping," Matt says with a thin smile. "Figured I'd take in the scenery. I assumed you all would sleep in more." He turns around. "This place is something else. I wonder how much money Tess's parents have. There's seriously nothing around here. I walked for like forty minutes and up a little bit of a cliff and saw only one house, but like, way out there."

"Matt," I say, trying to get his attention. "We need to leave here."

"What? Why?"

Cole suddenly appears through the brush, a wide grin on his face. "There you are," he says to Matt. He walks up to him and pats him on the back. "You had us all worried." Cole looks at me for a moment. "We had to send out a search party."

CHAPTER 28

I walk slowly behind Cole while he has his hand wrapped around Matt's shoulder. The two of them walk across the beach, laughing about whatever they're talking about.

My mind is racing a hundred miles an hour.

I'm not sure what I was thinking when I couldn't find Matt. Somehow my imagination ran wild. I thought the worst had happened. I thought...

I'm not even sure.

This is all IWriteAlone's fault. They start emailing me and I lose myself again. How much longer am I going to let a stranger control me? This stranger knows where I am, though. How can that be? How can they possibly know where I am? I think about the girl from the hotel lobby, who I saw again at the town's grocery store. Could IWriteAlone be her?

What if it's someone I know? Someone at the house I'm staying at? I think of Cole, Tess and even my own fiancé. I feel like I'm going insane. An image of Cole and his cocky smirk that was plastered on his face when I was scared about Matt. He sincerely seemed to enjoy watching me.

My gut is telling me there's more going on with Cole. Perhaps even Tess. I look at my fiancé as he laughs so freely with him.

I don't know who IWriteAlone is, but they spooked me. They know where I am, and I can't be here anymore. It's time to leave.

I watch Cole as he tightens his grip on my fiancé's shoulder, He leans in, and they start talking in hushed voices. What are the two talking about now? Matt glances back at me for a moment.

What is Cole saying to Matt?

Matt suddenly stops in his tracks. "You're really limping," he says. He walks up to me and grabs my hand. "Let's take a look at that leg." He looked at it before we started walking, but since I'm lagging so far behind, he must be worried. He doesn't know that the main reason why is that I want as much distance between me and Cole as I can get.

I don't trust him. I'm not sure I can trust anyone.

Matt whistles and waves Cole over. "It's a good thing we have a resident doctor available. Cole, take a quick look at this. Does she need anything? Bandages? I'm sure you've got some at your place."

Cole takes a few steps closer to me. He tilts his head. "Minor wound. No biggie. Band-aid it if you like."

Matt laughs. "Band-aid? That's it?"

Cole nods and raises his eyebrows. "Sure. People overreact about minor stuff. Rub dirt in it. That's what our ancestors did." He laughs and starts walking down the beach.

Matt walks with me now, holding my hand as we head towards the lake house. "You're shaking," he says as he notices my hand trembling. "What happened?"

Cole looks back at me and waits for my response. "I'm okay," I say, and Cole looks ahead again.

I'm not sure how to describe the feelings I have right

now. My mind is still racing. I'm not sure what to believe or who to trust.

How does IWriteAlone know where I am?

Tess is waiting for us as we come back inside through the patio door. Matt, Tess and Cole sit at the dining table. The three of them start planning what we should do today. Cole mentions another fire at night and Matt agrees. Matt wants to swim again.

"Maybe another round of chicken fighting, hey Sidney?" Matt says, looking at me. "We have to beat the cheaters." When I don't smile or sit with them at the table, Matt's smile slowly turns to concern. Now Cole and Tess watch me as I take a few steps back, toward the stairs.

"I'm going to lay down a bit, okay?" I say. Matt looks at Tess and Cole and back at me, nodding slowly.

"Okay," he says.

As I walk up the stairs and hear Cole and Matt laugh, I wonder if it's at my expense. *Is the crazy writer having another meltdown?*

Am I?

I can't stay here anymore. Matt doesn't know everything. He doesn't know about IWriteAlone emailing me. If I tell him and he doesn't agree to go, I'll leave without him. I'm emotionally drained.

The two men laugh hard again. The sound frustrates me more. How can they be having fun?

I'm halfway up the stairs when I realize I can't pretend any longer. It's time to leave and I don't care if I have to make another scene to get what I want.

"Matt," I call out. The laughter stops momentarily. "Can you come upstairs for a moment? I just want to talk."

Cole laughs. "I've heard that before. You're in

trouble, buddy."

CHAPTER 29

Matt slowly walks up the stairs behind me. We wait to talk until we're in the guestroom and the door is shut.

When I turn to Matt, he holds my hand tight. "What are you doing?" he asks. "Cole says you freaked out on him again."

I take a deep breath. "Is that what Cole said?"

Matt gestures for me to lower my voice. "Can you stop making a scene?" he scoffs. "Yesterday was great, well, most of it. When you exploded on Cole and Tess, I couldn't believe it. Now... you're doing it again. Why? Because I went on a hike?"

"IWriteAlone emailed me again."

Matt raises an eyebrow. "When?"

"Late last night. They attached an image of the grocery store we went to yesterday. IWriteAlone is following me again. She knows where I am." I cover my face. "I can't do this again. I can't."

Matt stands beside me and guides me to sit on the bed. "I thought you were done going on your email? We talked about not using it."

I nod my head. "I emailed Vanessa about the book I'm writing. I wanted to send some of it to her. Let her know that I can finish this story on time. I wouldn't have to give back the advance."

Matt purses his lips. "And you saw IWriteAlone's

email when you did?" I nod again. "That's... I'm sorry. How can they know where we are, though?"

I take another deep breath. "I don't know. When I saw the email and couldn't find you, I thought... I don't know. I thought terrible things."

"What? Like I was dead or something?" He laughs.

"It's not funny."

He stops and rubs my back. "Sorry, love. You really have an imagination, though. I just went for a walk." He leans into me. "All you drunks were still asleep... So why did you freak out on Cole?"

I look away. "I don't know. What if IWriteAlone is him? Or Tess? I'm just scared. I feel like a cornered animal or something. I can't think straight. I saw that email and couldn't find you... and lost it."

"What about that lady from the grocery store? You said you got a bad vibe from her when you ran into her in the hotel lobby."

"I don't know anymore. I just can't be here. I want to leave, Matt. I'm obviously not able to stay here."

Matt nods. "I'll talk to him."

I smile and kiss him. "Thank you."

"Why?" He laughs.

I take in a deep breath. "For understanding. I thought you'd make this hard for some reason."

"I think we've overstayed our welcome," Matt says, kissing my forehead. "I'll talk to Cole. We'll figure this out."

I nod. "Okay. Thanks."

"Stop thanking me," he says. "I'm your husband-to-be. You're upset. I got this." He smiles.

"What if they email again? Last time, IWriteAlone would send multiple emails. There could be more since I last checked. What if they took a picture of this house? Or the lake or beach? What if—"

"Stop, Sidney," Matt says in a hushed voice. "It's going to be okay. Don't open your emails, okay? You don't have to check them anymore."

I breathe out slowly. I need to know if there've been more messages, but I know Matt's right. Don't look at the account. I'll only work myself up. I remember how I was last year, refreshing my emails late at night, wondering if the stalker was nearby.

I think of Vanessa.

"Well, maybe I can have you check my emails for me. I need to know if Vanessa messaged me back."

Matt shakes his head. "Why would you care if she did?" He shakes his head again. "Why are you going to keep doing this to yourself?"

"The advance!" I shout. "My book. I know I can finish it this time."

"And what happens if it breaks you again?" I turn my head as if that will help me not hear the words he'll say next. "Sidney, I was so happy when you decided to just give this up. Now you're doing it again and you're already acting like how you were." He pauses before continuing. "Don't tell me you're wanting to leave here to work more on your book."

I shake my head. "No, Matt! I'm scared, okay?" He wraps his arms around me. "I'm scared," I repeat.

"Okay," he says. "Let's leave."

CHAPTER 30

I follow Matt as he goes back down the stairs. Cole and Tess are speaking quietly at the table between themselves until they see him.

"Hey guys," Matt says shyly. "Listen, we're both very thankful for you guys going out of your way to pick us up at the hotel and let us stay a few nights at your beautiful place, but I think we're going to head out."

"Leave?" Cole says, surprised. He looks at Tess. "What did I tell you?"

"You guys have been nothing but great hosts," Matt says, raising his hands in surrender. If he knew what happened last night, I wonder if he'd feel the same. The hosts invited me to their bedroom.

"What did we do?" Tess asks.

"Nothing," Matt says with a thin smile. "We had a blast. So much fun. We'll have to do it again sometime."

Cole stands up and scoffs. "I'm not sure I believe that one, bud." He walks over to the fridge and takes out a beer. "Want one?"

I stop myself from speaking up. Matt has this. Let him talk it out with Cole. How can he be drinking? I want to leave, and Cole is serving beer?

"I'm okay." Matt waves him off. "Thanks, though. Listen, Cole, I don't want to bother you for a ride. We'll call for an Uber."

Cole snaps off the cap and takes a long drink of his beer. He wipes his mouth with his hand. "Why do you both suddenly want to leave?" He looks at his girlfriend. "Sidney is about to accuse us of something again, isn't she, Tess?" Tess turns her head and stares out the window, trying to avoid getting involved.

Cole waves his hand in the air. "What should I say? I knew you were going to do this again. I'm not this stupid email person. IWrite-something... If I was an internet stalker I'd have a much cooler name. Something more ominous. IWriteAlone?" He looks around, but nobody is finding his humor funny at the moment.

"No, no, man," Matt says, trying to calm the situation. "We're not saying anything like that. The stalker emailed Sidney again."

I suddenly find my voice. "IWriteAlone sent me an email with an image of the grocery store we went to." I watch Cole's eyes as I say it to see if he gives any hint of what he's thinking. He takes another sip of beer and I feel lost. Tess still looks like she's about to burst into tears.

"Scary, right?" Matt asks. It's rhetorical, of course, but Cole answers it anyway.

"Sure, but why leave?" he says. "Stay here. You got two big dudes with you here. No one will mess with you, Sidney."

"She's had a hard time," Matt says, answering for me. "The hotel room. Now the email. It's a lot. We just want to go, guys."

Cole takes another drink of his beer, glancing at his girlfriend. Tess continues to stare outside, pretending that she's not in the room with us.

"Fine! Whatever. I think we've had enough of this fun weekend with you as well," he says mockingly.

"Cole!" Tess says, still looking out the window.

"No, Tess," he says. "We've been nothing but good to them and this is the thanks we get." He raises a finger. "Lobster dinner." He raises another. "Free stay at our place." Raises a third. "Use of our private beach. What else—"

"Cole," Tess says, now looking at her boyfriend. "Let's—"

"No, Tess," he says, whipping the beer bottle across the room. It smashes against the wall. I jump and scream. Tess covers her mouth, her eyes wide. Even Matt looks startled. His mouth gapes open and his hands are frozen in front of him.

"Come on, man," Matt pleads. "We don't want any trouble."

Cole shakes his head. "Pack your shit. Get out of my house."

CHAPTER 31

Matt zips up his case and looks at me. "Make sure you don't forget anything. We're not coming back here."

Finally, we're on the same page. I continue to fold my clothes neatly into my bag. Matt stuffs his in.

I know he wants to leave immediately but I'm not sure I'm ready to be inside a car with Cole after what happened. Matt said he'd rather Cole not drive us, but with no cell service and Cole being difficult, maybe it's best we not push this.

Maybe by the time we go downstairs, he'll have cooled off.

"I got a few things in their bathroom," Matt says. "Do you have anything in there? Hair curler or whatever?"

I shake my head. "I'm ready to go."

Matt leaves the room and I look out into the hallway. Part of me wants to jump in the car and hightail it out of this place, even if it means Cole's behind the wheel. Then I think of the computer in the office. What if IWriteAlone sent something new? What if they're outside the lake house now? What if they share something that tells me more about who they may be? I stand up and look out the window. Through the thick trees, I see the blue of the lake.

What if IWriteAlone is watching me right now?

I can't handle not knowing. I quickly go across the

hallway to the office and close the door behind me. As always, it takes forever for the computer to open. I sign in under the guest profile and log into my email.

The window on the screen turns white and takes forever to load. I breathe in deep to try and calm my pulse. I look down at my hands and both are trembling. I didn't even notice they were. It's as if my body is acting on its own now.

The screen finally loads, but the office door opens. Matt walks in and makes a face.

"What are you doing?" he asks. "We're leaving. Let's just go."

"I need to know if they've sent an email," I say. "What if they sent another photo? What if they're here?"

Matt covers his mouth. He's not angry at me for checking. In fact, he's on the verge of tears himself now.

"I'm sorry, love," he says. He clears his throat. "Let's go. I'm with you. You're safe."

The screen loads. I breathe out when I don't see an email from IWriteAlone. They only sent one. Just one. How unlike them. Typically, they would send me so many emails I'd be on the verge of madness. Now, I'm more paranoid that they aren't sending me anything.

There is one new email, though, from Vanessa. I click on it, reading it quickly. She wants to talk and asks me when we can.

"Well," Matt says. "Anything?"

I shake my head. "Just from Vanessa." I click reply and start to message her. I notice Matt getting more and more impatient.

"Really, Sidney?" he says. "You can email her at the hotel when we have wi-fi again."

I ignore him and type a quick reply. I let her know I'll

give her a call in a few hours.

I look up at Matt. "Done."

He nods his head slowly. "I'm ready. Do you have everything?"

I look down and try to think. Anything that's important is already in my baggage. Anything I've forgotten I'm fine with never seeing again.

I notice the drawer. There was a gun sitting on top of a pile of paperwork. I could take it with me.

The rational side of me clicks in. Why would I do that? We're leaving. It may not even be loaded. Matt would think I'm unhinged if I brought a gun into the car with us.

"I'm ready," I say to Matt.

The two of us head down the stairs. Matt carries both our bags down the steps. When we get to the ground floor, Tess is holding a broom and is cleaning up the mess Cole made with the beer bottle.

She turns to us and looks down at her feet. "Cole's waiting for you outside," she says.

"Thanks, Tess," Matt says. "Well... take care." He rolls our luggage across the floor and heads outside.

I walk toward the door, watching Tess continue to sweep the broken glass. Part of me wonders what will happen to her after we leave. Will Cole's frustrations be directed towards her?

How many more of Cole's messes will Tess be cleaning because of his rage after we're gone? Or worse, how many bruises?

It's hard to imagine the fun-loving Cole that Matt and I met at the restaurant hurting Tess. But I'm also coming to terms with how aggressive the current Cole is too. It's as if someone flicked a switch on his mood.

He truly is not the man I remember.

I'm at the front door and about to leave when I turn to Tess. "Hey," I say to her. She looks up at me. "If you ever need anything from me, let me know." I'm not even sure why I say it. I think I confuse Tess herself, who slowly nods in response.

It's not like I can say thanks for the weekend, but I'm also worried about her.

She gives me a thin smile. "Take care, Sidney." With one hand holding the broom, she gives me a small wave.

I breathe in deep as I leave the lake house, hopefully forever. How could a weekend end up so terrible?

Matt puts both the cases in the trunk and closes it. Cole's leaning against the car. He slicks back his curly hair with his hand and fixes the dark sunglasses on his nose. If I didn't think he was a complete lunatic, he would look very handsome, sexy even. His personality destroys the illusion.

"Are we ready?" Cole asks with a nasty tone. Great. He's still upset. Now we're going to be stuck in the car with him for over an hour. Maybe if we stop somewhere along the way, Matt and I will find a new ride to the airport. Cole won't be as aggressive in public, I hope.

Matt nods his head. "Thanks again, Cole. No hard feelings, right?" He goes to shake his hand, but Cole doesn't reach out. Instead, Cole lets Matt's hand stay in the air.

He lowers his sunglasses and looks at Matt. "No hard feelings." He shakes his hand hard before letting go. "Let's go."

I get in the back seat on the passenger side. Matt opens the front passenger door. I would have rather he sat in the back with me, but with how delicate the mood is right now, it's probably better he sits in the front with Cole.

The two did just shake hands, though. Maybe the next hour-plus of driving won't be as bad as I suspect.

Cole walks around to the driver's side of the car but doesn't get inside. Instead, he looks down and bends out of sight.

"What is he doing?" I ask, but Matt doesn't answer, looking outside as well to see.

I lean closer to the driver's side window to see but my seatbelt is holding me back. Suddenly Cole jumps back up, nearly making me scream.

Cole smiles at my expression and takes off his sunglasses. He waves at Matt.

"What the hell is he doing?" Matt says. He opens the door and walks around the car. I see the two talking. I sit for a few moments, waiting for them to both get inside. When I realize it's not happening, I know something's wrong. I take off my seatbelt and get out.

"Change of plans," Cole says, a smirk on his face. When I walk around, I see for myself why.

Both the driver's side tires are completely flat.

CHAPTER 32

"You don't have a spare?" Matt asks.

"Sure do," Cole says. "One."

I shake my head. "I can't believe this."

Cole turns to me with a smug look. "Can't believe what?"

I shake my head again. "We're about to leave and suddenly the tires are flat."

Cole shakes his head this time. "Not flat. Look for yourself." He points at the tire closest to him.

Matt bends to take a look. "It's been slashed."

"Both of them," Cole says, maintaining eye contact with me, his beady eyes seeing how I react to his words.

I look away. "How can this be happening?" I try to calm myself and look back at him.

Cole grunts. "Don't even start with me again. You've accused me of being anything and everything this weekend, and now you look at me like I've done something. Stop!"

"Let's just take a deep breath, everyone," Matt says, trying to calm the situation. "Let's think about this."

"Well, unless you want to hike for several hours or more, we're all a little stuck right now," Cole says.

Matt turns to him. "We must be able to do something about this, right?"

Cole smiles at him. "Guys, I'll call a tow. There's a guy

in town. There's only one tow around here, but how many people will need it? He'll come, repair or get me new tires, and off we'll go."

Matt nods. "Okay. Thanks." He looks at me and takes a deep breath. I'm sure he's noticing how on the verge I am of having a complete panic attack. "It's okay, Sidney," he says. "We'll sort this out and leave soon." For a change, I notice fear in Matt's eyes. He looks pale himself at what's happening.

"Few hours at most," Cole says. He turns to Matt. "Do you have a credit card or cash on you?"

Matt lets out a single laugh of confusion. "You want me to pay?"

Cole nods in response. "Do you know how many slashed tires I had before you two stayed with us?" He points to me. "This is your little stalker, isn't it? It's obvious. This happened because of you."

"Don't point at me!" I shout.

"Easy!" Cole says.

Matt puts up his hands again, pleading for us all to get along. "Guys, come on."

"You come on!" Cole shouts. "Your psycho fiancée is the one who needs to relax."

"Don't talk to her like that," Matt says, lowering his hands and looking at Cole intensely.

"What the hell did you say?"

"Cole!" Tess shoots from the front door. "Just stop."

Cole looks at me, then at Matt. "This is just not worth it." He starts walking toward the house. "Tow will be on its way soon."

CHAPTER 33

Matt and I head back upstairs with our baggage. Once we're inside the bedroom, he closes the door.

"What do we do now?" he asks.

I quietly look around the room. "There's more you need to know." It's time I tell my fiancé everything that's been happening this weekend.

Matt puts a finger to his lips. "Not here," he says in a hushed voice. "Outside."

"Outside?" I repeat. "What about IWriteAlone? The tires. What if they're out there now?"

Matt puts a finger to his lips again. "Just follow me. It's okay."

I agree, and as we head down the stairs, Cole and Tess are whispering to each other as well. They stop when they see us.

"We're going to go for a hike," Matt says.

Cole nods. "Have fun."

Matt grabs my hand and guides me out the front door. As we leave, I notice Cole glaring at me. His light blue eyes lock with mine.

We wait to talk until we're on a trail and the lake house is nearly out of sight. As we hike, I quickly scan the woods for any trace of life besides Matt and me.

"Sorry," he says. "I know you're scared, but I don't want to talk in that house. I feel like they can hear us or something."

"What are we going to do?"

"I don't know," Matt says.

"How long do you think a tow truck will take?"

Matt gives me a look. "There isn't going to be a tow truck, Sidney. It's him. He slashed the tires."

"Cole? I don't know what to make of any of this. So now you think Cole's IWriteAlone?" I ask.

Matt looks just as afraid as me as he grips my hand. It's usually Matt who has to calm me down. Now it's him who looks like he's seen a ghost.

"I don't know," he says. "I don't know what's happening here, but he's not telling us everything. Something's wrong."

I take a deep breath, trying to make sense of it. "It must have been Cole who trashed our hotel room," I say. "Tess was at the lake house. I don't understand, though. All of this was just to get us to stay with them? Why?"

Matt lowers his head. "All I know is we need to leave, and we can't rely on Cole or Tess to help us." He looks up at me. "You said you had more to tell me."

I purse my lips. "I'm not sure how helpful this is, but last night, Cole cornered me in the office when I was using the computer. He seemed agitated, or something."

"The man is completely crazy," Matt says.

"Then Tess came into the office and asked if I wanted to join her and Cole in their bedroom."

Matt's eyes go wide. "She did what?"

I put my hands on him to try and calm him. "I went to our bedroom, though. Tess kept apologizing profusely, saying it was Cole who made her ask. I believe her."

"He wanted to sleep with you last night?" Matt says, trying to make sense of it all.

"When I woke up, I wanted to tell you. I wanted to leave this place. I checked my emails and found the email from IWriteAlone. When I saw the image of the grocery store, I was scared. IWriteAlone knows where we are again." I look around the woods. "I tried to find you, but you were gone. I thought the worst. My crazy thriller brain always jumps to the worst-case scenario."

Matt nods. "I'm starting to think the same."

I shake my head. "Let's just go."

"Where?" Matt says, looking around him. "We don't know where we're going."

"Follow the gravel road that leads to the lake house," I say. "Didn't we take a right from the road to get here? When we get to the road, we'll go left and hike until we get into that small town. Can't be too long to get there. A few hours."

"They have internet," Matt says. "Can't you order an Uber online?"

"I have no frigging clue, Matt," I say. "Let's just leave."

"You're all banged up," he says, pointing at my knee. "That hike this morning wiped me out too. What if we get lost? What if we get stuck in the dark out here?"

"We should just leave," I say to him.

He shakes his head. "Go on the computer. Make an excuse. Maybe say you're going to write some more before our ride gets here. When the Uber gets here, we scramble. What's Cole going to do? Slash their tires too?"

"Why do you think Cole slashed the tires? What if he's right and the stalker is here?" I ask.

Matt shakes his head. "Call it a gut instinct or whatever. Mine is yelling at me to leave this place as quickly and safely as possible."

I think of the desk. "There's a gun in one of the office drawers."

"What?" Matt says, surprised.

"I found it the other day when I was looking for a notepad. I don't think it's Cole's. It must be Tess's father's gun. It's his office."

Matt nods. "Is it loaded?"

"I didn't touch it, Matt," I say. "I just found it."

He clears his throat. "Okay. When we get back, use the computer. Call us a taxi, Uber or anything. Whatever you can find online. Take the gun and give it to me."

"You want to take it with us when we leave?" I ask.

"Just a safety precaution," Matt says. "Maybe I'm overthinking this, and this is all just a misunderstanding. If not, and Cole really doesn't want us to leave, we'll have something to protect ourselves. I feel strongly he's up to something. I won't use it. Only if he makes me… Let's go."

As we head back to the house, Cole and Tess come into view. Without hearing what they're saying, I can tell it's heated. Tess is covering her face. Cole is waving his hands in front of her, animated as he talks.

"What are they doing now?" Matt asks.

"I don't know," I say. "What if Tess came with us?"

CHAPTER 34

Cole spots us walking up the treeline and heads back through the patio door. Tess looks towards us. She lowers her head and follows Cole inside.

"Remember the plan," Matt says. I nod as we walk up the steps. When we step through the patio door, Cole is grabbing another beer from the fridge.

How many has he had already today? It's not even past ten in the morning and he could already be intoxicated. Would he even be capable of driving us if the car was operable? He lets out a belch after taking a long drink. The answer is obvious.

Tess sits quietly at the dining table, alone, and does her best to not look at me or Matt.

I wonder what the two were talking about as we approached. With how irritable and drunk Cole is becoming, I worry how much worse this day will get.

Matt is already walking up the stairs, but I stop and face Cole. "How long for that tow?" I ask. I know his answer is going to be bullshit, but I just want to see what he says. Matt's giving me a disapproving look. This wasn't what we talked about.

Be lowkey. Call for a ride. Get out of here without instigating anything further.

Cole sighs. "I'm waiting for a response."

"You left a voicemail?" I ask.

He smiles. "No, an email."

"You emailed a tow?" Matt says, just as bewildered as me.

"How else?" he says. "I don't magically have cell service out here. None of us do."

"You don't have a landline?" I ask, confused.

Cole laughs. "No, we don't." He watches our expression as Matt and I look at each other. "Guys, we live out in the middle of nowhere and this is not my house. I think it's weird having the internet but no wired phone out here too, but what are you going to do? It's not my house." He laughs and takes another sip of his beer.

"Well," Tess speaks up, "Dad has a phone. I'm not sure where it is. I know they did some renovating."

"Shut up!" Cole shouts. Tess raises her shoulder and tries to hide within herself. "Tess, don't talk to these people. I told you; I'll handle it."

She looks away and back out the window.

I glance at Matt and worry things will escalate again, but he walks up to me and places his arm around my shoulder. I can already tell what he's thinking.

Stick to the plan.

"Tess," I say to her. She turns her head away from the window. "Is it okay if I use your computer for a little bit? I figured I may as well write some more of my story while we wait for the tow." I glance at Cole and quickly back to Tess.

Tess gives me a thin smile. "Of course."

"You didn't ask me," Cole says, leaning against the fridge.

"It's her house," I say challengingly. Tess's eyes grow wide, and she looks at Cole. Matt seems frozen in place.

Cole smirks at me. "The tow may be a while," he

says. "You can write all day and night. Maybe you can share more about your story later too. Tess would love that." Suddenly, it's as if his whole demeanor changes and softens.

I smile at them both as I head upstairs, with Matt following behind me.

CHAPTER 35

As soon as I enter the office, I lock the door behind me. I'm not sure how long it will take for me to figure out a way to get us a ride, but I don't want Cole or Tess to step in.

As I log into the computer, I can't stop thinking about what's happening. Did Cole slash the tires? If so, why? If he's really scheming something, why would he let me use his computer? Or could it be Tess? Is she hiding something that I don't know?

Are Cole and Tess working together? What if IWriteAlone is not one person, but two?

Cole says he never knew that I was an author. He had a stack of my books in his room, though. He said he bought them at the conference, but maybe that was a lie. Cole has lied so much in the short amount of time I've spent with him.

We should have left while we could. Matt didn't like the idea of hiking without any supplies or a plan. I don't care about our bags. If we're truly in danger, we should leave now. Grab a few bottles of water and some food and hit the road.

Cole didn't seem to care that we wanted to go on a hike before. Maybe he'll feel the same if we go again, only this time with supplies.

I think of Matt as well. It was only after he saw

the slashed tires that he finally came around and started getting worried. Why did it take so long? We knew the stalker was back in our life and was nearby. The picture of the grocery store in the email proved it. Now that the tires have been slashed, it only makes sense to be upset.

Cole certainly was. He demanded money for the damage the stalker did.

Nothing makes any sense. Me still being at this lake house least of all. Matt had a plan though, and of course I listened.

We should have just left. We should have gone. Why did I ever agree to come back inside?

I think of the stalker. IWriteAlone. What if I have it all wrong? What if it truly is a stranger doing this to me? The woman from the hotel lobby, or some stranger that figured out where I was staying after we checked out?

Thankfully the computer desktop finally loads. I open a browser. I need to figure out a way to get a ride for us. If I can't get one, we're leaving here immediately. I don't care how much Matt hates the idea of hiking around some place we've never been before. We need to go, before it's too late.

Then again, if the stalker is a stranger and is watching us, they will follow. And worse, they have a weapon. The tires were slashed with something sharp enough to cut through thick rubber. What if we leave and the stalker follows us?

I remind myself we'll be armed. I open the desk drawer and confirm the gun is still there. I close the drawer and continue with the plan.

I start to type the address for Uber's site. I figure that will be the best way to try and get a ride arranged online, although I'm not sure how to use it. Isn't it just an app you use on the phone? Neither Matt or I have ever used it before.

My fingers start to tremble. I try to calm myself, but I know I'm scared. No matter how many breathing exercises I try, my body will react even with me trying to control it.

What if the stalker is watching me right now? The office window is wide open. Someone with binoculars could easily look inside the room... at me. I stand up and close the drapes and sit back down.

I can't help myself now. I need to know. IWriteAlone isn't one to stay quiet for long. They will have sent more emails. I need to know if they have. I need to know what they have planned.

I log into my email account and wait patiently for the screen to load. When it does, I let out a breath.

Nothing. No new emails. Only the one from the other day. I know I should be happy about this, but I'm more nervous.

What if IWriteAlone can't send anymore emails to me because they're here, at the lake house? I don't have any wi-fi here. The stalker wouldn't either. The only way to send an email is through this computer.

I can feel my heart beating faster with every thought. I can't lose my cool. I need to stay present. I have a gun now. If anything happens, Matt and I will be safe.

No more looking at my emails. Matt is right. The more I do, the more anxious I get. I click on my profile to log off. When I do a drop-down menu appears showing other users' emails. Cole has one: Colemurphy123. But it's the email above Cole's that has my attention.

IWriteAlone2009.

The stalker isn't outside this house. I've been living

with them this past weekend.

Tess?

Cole has an email on here, but not Tess. Then again, it could be a second profile Cole's created. I look down at the drawer with the gun. Part of me wants to grab it and run downstairs and demand answers.

I think of Matt. If there's a way for me to arrange for a ride, we need it. Matt can hold the gun until the ride is here and we leave. Once we're in town, we'll call the police.

I can't believe it. Cole. Tess. How could I be so stupid? I thought the invitation from Cole to come to his lake house was a little much. We weren't very close when we were younger. We dated for less than a month. He was only my tutor for a few months.

He wanted me to come to his house. It's remote. There's no way for me to run. What do Cole and Tess have planned?

Cole must have destroyed our hotel room to scare me into wanting to leave.

I look down at my hand and I'm surprised to see it's no longer trembling. I'm too angry to be afraid. My whole life was ruined because of the stalker. Now I know who it may be. Cole or Tess. Or both. I think of the gun again. I should scare them the same way IWriteAlone got to me.

I click the stalker's profile. Of course it doesn't just let me into their account. A password is required. I'll try a few random ones. Tess1234. Lakehouse456!

Nothing is working. I wonder how many tries I have until the account locks itself.

I can almost hear Matt's voice, demanding I stick with the plan. Find a ride. Get the gun. Leave here.

I can't stop myself, though. For the past year

IWriteAlone has had full control over my life. My life was turned upside down because of them. Now, they're in this house, and I have a gun.

I think of Matt again. He was so drastically different after the slashed tires. He didn't seem so worried about hiking in the woods even though IWriteAlone could be out there.

I purse my lips and slowly type in another password. When I hit enter, I pray I'm wrong.

I'm not.

The account opens and I now have access to the email account of IWriteAlone2009.

My eyes begin to water as I see the history of emails my stalker sent to me. All of them, including the one from early this morning.

I look down at the drawer and consider taking the gun. If I do, I'm scared I'll use it on him now that I know the truth.

I stand up from the desk and storm across the hallway into the guest room. Matt's sitting on the bed. When I enter the room, he smiles at me.

"Did you find a way to get a ride?" he asks.

I don't answer him. I'm trying to find the words. I'm not sure if I'm about to cry or scream. I settle for rage instead.

"It was you!" I shout.

CHAPTER 36

"I can't believe it!" I scream. "You!"

Matt stands up from the bed, his arms raised. "What are you saying, love?"

"Don't you *love* me! You're the stalker!"

"What?" he says, giving me his best confused face. Give this man an Oscar. He's played me like a fiddle for the past year and I had no idea.

"IWriteAlone's profile was on the computer," I say. "When I found it, I tried to log on. Guess which password I used? You always use the same password for everything, Matt, even your stalker profiles."

Matt lowers his hands and his face drops. "I can explain. I—"

"Explain?" I shout. "You ruined me! You scared me to death, pretending to be a stalker. You made me believe someone was following me. Out to get me. You harassed me with your emails, making me worry for my life. But, please, explain. Why?"

Matt lowers his head. "I never meant for it to be this way."

"What did you mean it to be, Matt?"

He glances at me, and I'm sure all he can see is the anger in my eyes. "Your career was killing us. Why couldn't you see? You put your writing above me. You pushed back the wedding. You didn't care anymore! Once

I started emailing you as IWriteAlone, I thought I could get you to realize somehow what you were doing. Make you realize what we had. Finally, you stopped writing, and we were better again."

I scoff. "Better again? I could barely leave the house."

Cole's distant voice echoes through the hallway from downstairs. "You guys okay up there?"

"No, we're not, Cole!" I shout while staring at my fiancé. "The past year has been hell for me. How could you do this to me? Because you were scared I was going to leave you?"

"After you stopped, we got better."

"Better?" I say, surprised. "You made out with that girl from work."

Matt lowers his head again. "I told you about it that night. I couldn't keep that a secret from you."

"But you had no trouble not telling me it was you who ruined my life as my stalker? If you did it all for me, why did you cheat?"

"I was upset at everything. After what happened, you were different. I tried to encourage you to take the counselling the publisher offered but you refused."

I let out a singular *ha*. "So, your response to me going through a breakdown over the trauma you caused me was to make out with someone else?"

Matt ignores me. "I love you, Sidney. I just wanted to marry you. I don't care that you've become some famous writer. None of that matters to me. I want us to be together and happy. Writing was making you miserable. Long nights. All the rewrites with the publisher. All the demands they made for tours. You were becoming someone else."

I shake my head. "So you tried to make me into

something you could control." I grind my teeth and clench my fist. "I can't believe you. You used IWriteAlone to control me." As I say the words it dawns on me. "And you wanted to control me again. When you saw me start writing again, suddenly IWriteAlone sends another email."

Matt glances around the room, trying his best not to look at me. "I didn't mean for this to get out of control."

"You didn't care how much IWriteAlone ruined me. I almost gave up something I love doing because of what you did. I would tremble uncontrollably at the idea of the stalker. I could barely function as a person because of you. I nearly lost my sanity, and it was all because of you. Because you wanted to control me."

"I just wanted you to love me," Matt says, reaching out for me.

I take a deep breath and stare at my fiancé. His eyes watery. His arms reaching out for me. Usually, I'd love nothing more than to feel his embrace. Take in his warmth. Feel his love.

It was all a lie.

I take a step forward and slap him hard enough that his face turns. He covers his cheek and looks at me, shocked. I wiggle the ring off my finger and throw it at his feet.

"We're done."

CHAPTER 37

"What's happening up here?" I turn and see Cole standing at the door.

"I'm done with everyone." I walk up to Cole, but he doesn't move. "Get out of my way," I say coldly.

He listens this time. He steps back and I walk out of the room, down the hallway.

"Where are you going?" Cole asks.

"I need a drink," I say as I head down the stairs.

I pass by Tess in the kitchen. She stares at me, wide eyed. "Is everything okay?"

I take a deep breath. "No, it's not." I can feel my eyes watering. "Is it okay if I get a bottle of wine?" Tess looks at me, shocked. She doesn't answer. I'm sure whatever look of rage and tears is on my face is enough to put anyone off.

I walk past her and go down the stairs. A faint smell of dust hits me when I look around the unfinished basement. Stacks of boxes form a path that leads to the wine cellar.

As I pass by one of the boxes, I notice a wireless phone in it. I smile. Of course the phone was downstairs.

That doesn't matter anymore. I push against the wooden doors of the wine cellar. The room is dimly lit with mahogany shelves filled with bottles.

Tess said her parents were doing some renovations and I wondered what she meant. As beautiful as the house is, with a luxurious spot on the lake, everything inside the house was sort of dated: the wood-paneled walls upstairs in the bedrooms and the wallpapered kitchen.

Looking at the newly installed wine cellar, I can see where her parents started the renos.

When I open the cellar door, a stench hits me. Unbearable. I want to leave but instead look for a bottle of wine. I'm not leaving without something to drink.

The cellar door opens again. I turn and see Matt. His face is pale. As soon as he steps inside, he covers his face.

"It reeks," he says. He looks at me. "I'm sorry. I know that's not enough. I know you don't trust me."

"I will never trust you... ever again."

He takes in my words. "I get that. I want us to talk more about this when we get back to town."

I scoff. "There's nothing to talk about, Matt. It's over."

"Did you call for a ride?"

"Help yourself," I say, examining some of the bottles. I find one that has a bunch of dust on it. I slide it out from the rack and look at the label. It looks old, fancy and it's a cabernet sauvignon. Perfect. "There's a phone in one of the boxes in the basement. Make a call yourself."

"And the gun?"

Of course, the wine isn't one I can twist off. Part of me wants to bash it against the cellar rack to open it and have a taste. I look around at some of the other bottles, hoping I can find one that I can open. I don't want to look around Tess's kitchen for an opener.

"I didn't get the gun, Matt, but you know where it is."

Matt takes a step towards me. "We need to leave here."

"I don't care what you do," I say. I take out a bottle from the rack, and to my relief, it's one I can open. I quickly screw off the top and take a sip.

"Something is wrong here," Matt says.

"A lot of things are wrong," I say. I turn to him. "I get it now. No wonder you weren't scared of IWriteAlone finding us in the woods. You slashing the tires is a bit much." I take another sip from the bottle, making a sour face when I'm done.

"I didn't slash the tires."

I turn to him. "How can I even believe you? You're trying to manipulate me still. Control me. Scare me some more. I'm done being scared. I'm done being with you."

Matt's face looks even more pale. His mouth gapes open. I stare at him, rage filling my eyes, and can't understand why he's not even looking back. His eyes grow wider as he continues to stare behind me.

I turn and realize what has his attention.

Sticking out of the rack from the empty slot where I grabbed a bottle of wine is a hand.

CHAPTER 38

I take a closer look. The hand is pale but the skin at the top of the fingernails is dark. The arm leads to an area between the back wall and the wine rack. When I peer through the rack, I see a face. A larger man with a thin mustache. I recognize him immediately from the photos.

"It's Tess's dad," I say. I look closer and through the bottles and wood see a second body. "It's her mother too."

I look back at Matt. He's still wide eyed but manages to speak. "What do we do?"

I breathe out. "The gun. Just like you said. We grab it. There's a phone in one of the boxes down here. Once we have the gun, we call 911."

"What if they have a gun already?" Matt says.

I lower my head. "It was still in the drawer when I was upstairs." We both look up at the ceiling as we hear footsteps cross the ground floor above.

"We need to act fast," I say. "You take care of Cole. If Tess comes close, I'll manage her."

"Take care of Cole?"

I hand him one of the wine bottles and grip one tightly myself. "Just keep him busy if you have to. I need enough time to get to the office."

Matt looks at me. Tears are coming down his face. "What is wrong with these people?" He takes a deep breath. "I'm sorry, Sidney. For everything… I love you."

I feel my stomach turn. I'm not sure if it's from fear or Matt's betrayal of me. It's all overwhelming. I think of the characters in my books. We need to keep level heads through this. Matt's already on the verge of losing it.

"We'll talk when we get out of here," I say. I open the wine cellar door, and Matt reluctantly follows behind me.

I gesture towards a box as we do. "There's the phone." Matt nods.

As we approach the stairs, I notice his hand is trembling so much that the wine bottle nearly falls from his loose grip. I put my hand over his. Our eyes meet. I take in a deep breath, and he does the same.

I want to say how much I love him. I want to tell him that we'll be okay. We'll find a way to leave here. I'm not sure if either of those statements are true.

I take the first step up the stairs and Cole appears in the doorway. He stares down at us and smirks.

CHAPTER 39

I glance back at Matt, who looks even more scared than me.

"Two bottles," Cole laughs. "A pair of alcoholics. I think I'll have to bill you for bottle service." Cole's grin widens as we climb the stairs.

Suddenly, Matt pushes me to the side and rushes Cole. He raises the bottle in his hand and bashes it down on Cole's shoulder, missing his head by a few inches. The bottle breaks, cutting Matt's hand. Cole shouts as his flesh opens and bleeds through his shirt. Matt, unfazed by his own wound, grips what's left of the broken bottle in his hand and tries to stab him.

Cole screams and grabs Matt's hand. Cole shoves Matt hard against the wall, nearly sending him tumbling down the stairs. Cole easily brushes Matt away from him. As Matt falls to the floor, I quickly run up the steps. Matt stands up quickly and slashes towards Cole with the bottle, opening a wound on Cole's hand.

Cole takes a step backwards, looking at the cut and touching his shoulder. "What are you doing?" he shouts. He wrestles the bottle out of Matt's fingers, pushing his digits backward until I hear an audible crack.

My mouth gapes open as my fiancé shrieks in pain. I look into the kitchen where Tess is just watching the two men, her face in just as much shock as mine. Beside her is a set of kitchen knives. I take a step towards her, and Tess puts her arms up to cover her face. Thankfully, she doesn't grab them.

"Upstairs!" Matt shouts at me. "Go!"

Before I can, Cole shoves Matt hard to the floor. As Matt falls, his leg twists against a side table. He screams in pain. Matt tries to stand up but can't.

Now Cole looks at me. I scurry up the stairs, but he chases me, grabbing me by the back of my shirt, pulling me down the stairs with ease.

"What are you doing?" he shouts. "What's wrong with you people?"

Matt's crawling on the floor. "My ankle!"

"He needs help," I say. "Please, let us go. Just let us leave!"

Cole laughs. "Just stop. Both of you." He looks down at his cuts. He laughs, somehow finding all this amusing.

"Just let us go," I say to Cole.

He looks at me but doesn't answer. "This has really gone too far," he says. He looks at Tess, whose face is just as panicked as mine.

Matt tries to stand but fumbles back to the ground and cries out.

"Don't kill us," I say.

Cole turns to me. A wicked smile growing on his face. "Kill you?"

I look at Tess. "Your parents. There in the wine cellar. Dead."

Tess looks at Cole. "What?"

Cole raises his eyebrows. He looks at his girlfriend and back at me. "I've had enough of you."

Tess covers her face and turns her back. Typical Tess.

"Tess," I shout to her. "Please!"

Cole tightens his grip on my shirt and pulls me across the room.

"Leave her alone!" Matt shouts from the floor.

I let out a breath. "He needs a doctor."

Tess laughs, her back turned, still looking out the window. It starts low, until she's full out belly laughing.

"Please," I say. Tess's laughter grows louder. Cole looks at her, just as confused as me.

She turns to me and glances at her boyfriend. "Cole, aren't you the doctor? Why don't you help poor Matt?"

Cole raises an eyebrow. "Tess, stop."

"Oh, I forgot," she says, tilting her head. "That was a lie." She steps closer to Cole and me. "You've told nothing but lies since I've met you!" She continues forward, pointing at Cole. "You didn't live up to anything you promised me!"

"Tess!" Cole shouts. "I'm dealing with this. We can still make this work." Cole looks at me again. "Did you say Tess's parents are in the basement?"

Suddenly Tess brings a large kitchen knife from behind her back. She runs up to Cole, grabs him by his shoulder and plunges the knife into his back repeatedly. Cole shouts and shrieks with every blow until he drops to the floor.

"Lies!" Tess shouts as she kicks his body on the floor. "Lies! Lies! Lies!" His body flinches and soon stops moving entirely. Tess brushes her hair with the red-stained knife. Blood drips from her fingers.

She looks up at me. "He was really starting to bother me."

CHAPTER 40

Tess leans her head back and shouts angrily. She starts kicking Cole's lifeless body over and over. "It was supposed to be a fun weekend, Cole! You said you knew her, Cole!" She stops to catch her breath. "Look at you now!" Tess hears Matt shifting on the floor. "Don't you move!" She raises the knife in the air, pointing it at him. "And you," she says, pointing it at me now, "don't do anything stupid. Cole brought this on himself with his lies. Don't join him."

Tess steps over Cole's body. I feel frozen as I watch Tess morph from a quiet, timid woman into a wicked killer.

I look at Matt, who has the same expression. Then he motions with his eyes towards the stairs.

Tess turns to me and smiles. "What are you hiding?" she asks. She puts the bloody knife to her chin as if in deep thought, leaving a stain of Cole's blood on her face. "What's upstairs?"

I find my wits and turn, about to run, when Tess shouts, "I'll kill him next!" I stop and look at Matt. "Don't think about it," she says.

I stop moving and lower my head. I plead with her, "Just stop this, Tess. We just want to leave. Find a doctor. We just want to go, okay?"

Tess is unmoved. "Come down the stairs." When

I don't move, she shouts, "Now!" Her timid voice is suddenly much deeper.

I do as she says. She uses the threat of the knife to guide me away from the stairway. "If you run, I'll kill your fiancé." She points the knife towards my chest. "Just don't run," she whispers. "Now, what are you hiding?"

I take in a deep breath. "We just want to leave."

"That's not happening right now," she says coldly. "Is it in your travel bags? What do you have?"

"Leave us alone!" Matt shouts.

Tess ignores him. "I'm going to find it, Sidney."

I look in her eyes and all I see are bright blue orbs of pure madness staring back at me. "Nothing," I say. Let her think it's in our bags.

Tess climbs a few stairs. "Both of you, follow me."

"My leg!" Matt shouts.

"Crawl!" Tess yells back.

Tess points the knife at my chest, letting Matt know she means it. He does what she demands and slowly moves towards the stairs. She guides us slowly up the stairway until we're in front of our bedroom door. She opens it and motions for Matt.

"Crawl to the bed," she says.

Again, Matt listens. She watches him carefully in case he tries to make a move. As he comes past us, Tess keeps the knife an inch from my chest. I can see in her eyes that she wouldn't think twice about plunging it into me.

When Matt's on the bed, Tess directs me to sit there as well. I lie beside Matt, holding him tightly.

Tess smiles as she enters our room. She continues to point the knife at us as she steps towards our luggage. She empties everything from both bags to the floor and starts to sort through it with her feet, watching us to ensure we're not moving.

Matt gestures towards the door. I know what he wants me to do. Run. Grab the gun. If I do, she could kill him. What if she gets to me before I can? It's too risky.

"What are you hiding?" Tess says. She breathes out deeply. She points the knife at me again. "I will figure it out, Sidney. You two are up to something."

"What are you going to do with us?" Matt says.

Tess gives a thin smile. "We're going to continue with what I always wanted to do. Have a great weekend together." She lowers the knife to her side and steps out into the hallway, closing the door behind her. I hear a click.

Did she lock the door?

I quickly get up from the bed and try the bedroom door, but it won't open. She's locked us in from the outside.

CHAPTER 41

We stay trapped inside the room for what feels like hours. Every so often we hear footsteps outside the door. She's searching for what she thinks Matt and I are hiding.

I wait for Tess to open the door with the gun in her hand and a wicked smile on her face. Thankfully, the creaks continue past our room.

The creaking becomes more distant as she heads down the stairs. I stand up from the bed and tug on the door, trying to open it. I know my effort is fruitless, but I don't know what else to do. Soon it will be nighttime.

Does Tess expect us to spend the night in our new prison? Will she give us food? Water?

Why is she even doing this to us?

After she murdered Cole in front of us, she yelled that he lied to her. That he claimed to know me better.

Whatever's happening, it's because of me that we are stuck here.

I look at Matt. As he lies in bed, he's soothing his leg, grimacing at just the slightest touch.

"How bad is it?" I ask.

He nods. "Bad. I sprained my ankle when I was a kid playing basketball. This is much worse. It could be broken." He purses his lips and stares at his leg, taking in his words, knowing he's powerless to do anything.

I try to open the door again and start pounding on

the door. "Let us out!"

"Just let it go," Matt says. He takes a deep breath and grimaces again.

I hear muffled sounds from outside. Short grunts coming from downstairs.

"What is she doing?" I say as I put my ear to the door. I hear more grunting sounds followed by multiple thuds. When the sounds stop, I take my ear off the door and look at Matt.

Light is shining through the tiny window. It's tight, but I think I can squeeze through it. I look down and remind myself why I ruled that out. It's a straight fall to the ground. We'll both have broken legs if I try. Tess will easily find me.

Besides, Matt won't be able to get through the window. Maybe it's worth a shot, though.

I turn to Matt. "If I can get through the window, I can sneak into the house and grab the gun. She hasn't found it yet. The longer we wait, the more chance she'll find it."

Matt gestures for me to be quieter. "No. Too risky."

"What then?" I say. "We can't stay here."

He lowers his head. "I'm so sorry, Sidney. I'm sorry." Matt's starting to break down now. He covers his face and shakes in the bed.

"Matt," I say as I sit beside him, "not now. We need to keep our heads if we're going to get out of this."

He looks at me. "I'm not going to make it."

"Stop! Yes, you are."

He lowers his head again. "If you find a way, you take it and run."

"I won't leave you," I say, caressing his chest. "We're going to get out of here." I grab his hand. "And then I'm going to seriously be angry with you."

He gives me a thin smile. "I don't deserve you. What I did to you was the worst a partner can do to someone they love. You're right. I was controlling you. Worse. Breaking you. I was thinking about myself. That's all I ever do. I deserve this... We wouldn't be here right now if it wasn't for me."

"This is not your fault. Cole did this. Tess. They planned this. From the moment we came to their house, they weren't going to let us go."

"I can't stop thinking of those bodies in the basement," Matt says. "She's going to put us down there too, isn't she?" I don't answer. "I'm so sorry, Sidney."

"We're going to figure this out. Don't lose faith. Not yet."

"She killed her own parents," Matt says, shaking his head in disbelief. "She murdered Cole. It's obvious that we're next. We're not leaving here."

"Stop it! We can—"

A knock at the door startles me. Both Matt and I freeze as it slowly opens. Tess is staring at me, the knife still firmly in her hand. I almost let out a sigh of relief knowing that she doesn't have the gun. There's still a chance. I just have to wait for my moment to get it.

"Sidney," she says in a soft voice. "We need to talk." She gestures for me to leave the room with the bloody knife. She looks at Matt. "Girls' talk. Sorry." As her grins widens, so do Matt's eyes. Tess is truly insane.

CHAPTER 42

Tess gestures for me to leave the room. Matt stares at me, wide eyed. He must be wondering the same thing I am. What can Tess want with me? Will I be coming back? Will I ever see Matt again?

I stand up from the bed and walk into the hallway. Tess keeps one hand gripped tightly on the kitchen knife, pointed at me, and shuts the bedroom door, locking it.

"Down the stairs," she demands.

I do what she says. Tess keeps the knife close to my back. I think of Cole and the shocked expression on his face as his girlfriend stuck him with it. Now she's behind me, likely just as willing to do the same.

I close my eyes as we get to the main floor. Cole's lifeless body is the last thing I want to see again. My heart quickens as I realize that I'll be joining him soon if Matt and I can't escape this place.

I open my eyes slightly to ensure I don't trip on his corpse. When I do, he's no longer on the floor. His body is gone.

A fresh citrus smell strikes my nose. A mop and bucket are against the wall. The water inside has a red tint to it. The wood floor is still wet at my feet.

"Let's talk in the living room," Tess says. "I brought up a bottle of wine." I don't move. I continue to look at the clean floors in shock. Only a few hours ago, a body was there. Cole's. Now he's gone. Like it never happened.

"Cole's in the wine cellar now," Tess says. I look up at her, surprised, and she grins back. "Please," she says, gesturing to the couches.

I look up the stairs. If I run to the office, I could lock the door and get the gun before she has a chance to catch me. Would I have enough time to get to Matt before she hurts him? The psychotic grin Tess is showing tells me she won't hesitate to kill again.

Even if I got to the gun, would I be capable of pulling the trigger?

I do as she says and sit on the couch. She sits on a lounge chair across from me, closer to the stairs.

"I'm glad we can finally talk," Tess says. "Ever since you came here, that's all I wanted to do with you. Talk. Get to know you. Get to know the master storyteller who came up with my favourite book. *My Life as a Killer.*" She shakes her head. "Your main character, Tracy, she was so inspirational."

Inspirational? The character was a murderer. She killed indiscriminately. You weren't supposed to root for her.

Tess raises her eyebrows. "I must say though, you got that part with the boiling sugar all wrong. A person doesn't die instantly with a pot of boiling sugar dumped on them. It takes a while, an excruciating while, to die from it. After I read that scene in your book, I had to try it for myself. The recipient likely wishes you had done better research and it was a quick death like you explained."

My mouth drops. Tess murdered someone the same way I described in my book? There were many murder scenes in that novel. How many other scenes did she try to recreate? My eyes widen when I realize she may test another on Matt or me.

"Still," she says playfully, "your inaccuracies didn't take away from the story, of course."

I take a deep breath. "So," I say, managing to find the words, "all of this is because of me?"

"Of course," Tess says. "Ever since I read *My Life as a Killer*, I knew I had to meet you."

"Why?"

Tess's grin fades. She looks down. "You are a master storyteller... I wonder, did you always write?"

I shake my head. "No. I started reading when I met Cole. True crime books mostly. I started writing my own stories much later."

"Cole got you into reading," Tess says with a thin smile. "I guess that was one thing he said that was true." She puts a hand on her chest. "I've been a storyteller for a long time. A very long time. Ever since I was a child, in fact. The people you found in the cellar are not my actual parents." She shakes her head. "No. My parents, they weren't the kind loving type. They hurt me. I would go to school and listen to stories from other students about what they did with their mother and father in awe. I never had the same experience." She smiles. "I didn't deserve that. I still remember how I would play with my dolls and make believe how a family was supposed to be. I'd have my Ken doll father, Barbie doll mother, and a smaller Barbie doll for me. When I was in my room, alone, I would pretend. Make up scenarios where the Barbie dolls had the perfect family. The perfect life together."

"Why are you telling me all of this?" I ask.

"I'm getting to that!" Tess shouts with a harsh tone. She softens immediately. "This is important." She shakes her head and stands up from her seat, then walks over to me, the knife pointing towards my face. She leans towards me and grabs a bottle of wine on the side table. It's already open. She pours two glasses, handing me one. She sits back in the chair and takes a sip.

"Go ahead," she says. When I don't, she laughs. "I didn't do anything to your drink, Sidney. You saw me pour it." I take a deep breath, trying to understand what's happening when she yells again. "Drink!" I quickly take a sip, watching her and the knife that's dangling in her hand.

I imagine throwing the glass of wine at her. It would be a good distraction. Would it give me enough time? The gun is so close but feels unreachable.

All I need is seconds, and I can get to it. How do I use it, though? For all my writings about crime, you would think I know how to properly handle a weapon.

"Where was I?" Tess says. "Right, my childhood. Bad parents. You get the gist. When I was eighteen, they couldn't stand me anymore. It was a mutual feeling. They kicked me out onto the street with nothing. Nothing! Who does that?" She scoffs. "I came back, though. I took care of them first. Police never found them. They never found me either. As far as they know, Tess Simmons disappeared with her family. Soon after, I found a new house to stay in. Unfortunately, people were already living in my new house, so they had to go. Police never found them either. I made up a new story of who I was, just like I did with my dolls. I acted like someone else. Made up a new life for myself. A new identity. Whenever I felt people were catching on to my lies, I'd move to a new town or city. Many stories later, I found this house. It was perfect. Two people lived here. Of course, they had to go. This was to be my new home. My new story. This Tess Simmons was different from the others." She looks over at the family photo of the couple who lived here and the small girl. I had assumed it was Tess in the picture. "I never met the little girl from the photo," Tess says. "I figured she'd come for a visit at some point, and I'd have to add another body to the cellar. But she never came... I guess she didn't like her parents either." She grins.

My bottom lip quivers at the idea. Just how many people has Tess killed? How many different pretend lives has she had? How many stories has she made up for herself?

"I knew I was a bad person," Tess continued. "What I was doing was wrong. No matter how much I committed to my new story, I knew that I wasn't right." She smacks the side of her head. "I even thought of putting an end to my story, permanently. Then I read your book. I became obsessed. Your main character, Tracy Macher. She was just like me. I understood her. I got it. And so do you. You wrote her. She was the main character, and you wrote her so well. It was like you understood what it was like to be something like me. That's when I knew we were meant to meet each other. I no longer felt sad. In my moment of doubt, when I was at my lowest, I found you. It was meant to be." Tess smiles.

"What was meant to be?" I ask.

"Us!" she exclaims. "After reading and rereading your book, I went online. I found out so much about you. I hoped to meet you in person, but you never did signing events. I never had the opportunity. I even wrote to you. I must have sent a dozen or so emails, but you never wrote back. I was disheartened. I looked up to you so much and hoped for just a small response. Anything."

She takes a deep breath. "I have to admit, I took that personally at first, but I was still obsessed with meeting you. I was very active on an online forum for fans of yours. One of the users caught my attention immediately. He said that you were close friends."

"Cole," I whisper.

Tess purses her lips. "I told you we met online. Cole and I private messaged each other for months. He was such an interesting man. He shared so many things about himself. He said you and him still spoke to each other. He said that he was a doctor. Wealthy. When we met in person, I couldn't believe what a catch Cole seemed to be." She glances toward the basement stairs. "So many lies, though." She takes a sip of wine and looks at me. "I found out he wasn't a doctor. Then he told me he was in med school. Found out that was a lie. Found out he was broke. Not a dime to his name." She scoffs. "But he told me he could arrange for us to meet. None of his lies mattered to me if that part was true. He even showed me a picture of you two from a photo booth that you took when you were younger. I believed him... The only thing he didn't lie about was his looks. He was handsome, but dumb. I could easily manipulate him by creating a story and playing the part. I was the shy Tess. A subservient woman who praised Cole for the lies he told me. I didn't mind playing the wallflower. He felt comfortable when he felt he was in control... I put up with a lot from him, so I could get to you." She takes another sip of wine and laughs. "I was starting to believe that the only use I had for Cole was when his clothes were off."

I think of how Tess murdered him so coldly. I cover my face. "I can't talk about him anymore. Please."

Tess smiles. "I was going to kill him. He had told me

lie after lie. He promised that he could get his close friend, you, to stay the weekend with us at the lake house. I believed him. We watched you at the convention. We saw your keynote speech. We monitored you at the hotel and where you went for dinner and joined you. Cole charmed you into sitting with us. He offered you to stay at the house… and you declined. I was so upset. We fought. He couldn't do the one thing he said he could. The only reason I had for keeping him around, and he failed. But then he told me you were coming!" Tess smiles. "Like I said, it was fate. But then you came to the house and it was evident that you weren't happy. You wanted to leave. Cole and I fought again. I could have killed him that night, but then the next day you agreed to stay. Even better, you started to write again, Write about me!" She shakes her head and grins. "Cole never knew about my past. Not my real past, at least. He never knew the real Tess Simmons. Only the one I made up. The fake me."

I bring the wine to my lips, taking a sip. Usually my hands would be trembling, but for some reason, they're not. They're steady as I take in all the terrible details Tess shares.

"Why am I here?" I ask. "Why are you telling me this?"

"For you to know the *real* me," she says with a smile. "You don't know what it means to me that you're here. The author who wrote Tracy Macher. A fictitious woman who helped me get through tough times. You didn't know what impact she had on me. Now, you're writing a story and using me as inspiration… but it's based on a lie." She takes a deep breath. "I need you to know who I really am. It will help with your book."

"My book? You're keeping me alive to write a story

about you?"

She nods. "Imagine what a real-life Tracy Macher would be like for readers. The world needs my story. You're the one to write it. It's meant to be, Sidney."

I think of the gun in the office drawer. "I can do that," I say. "What about Matt?"

"No harm will come to him," she says. "Not unless you want me to. Now that you know he was the one who ruined you, I can help you get even." She puts the edge of the knife to her lip. "I can do it for you."

I look down. "No. Don't hurt him."

"Fine," Tess says curtly.

"I can start now," I say.

She shakes her head. "No. You haven't done much research yet." She points the knife at me with a smile. "I know your process. First you spend months outlining and researching. We will have plenty of time for you to understand me. I read that you don't even write a sentence until you've outlined the whole book on a notepad first. Is that true?"

"I don't need any of that," I say. "I'm motivated to start writing now. Right now. Your words... inspired me."

Tess takes her glass of wine, wipes her head back and finishes the glass. She stands up from the couch, the knife in her hand, and gestures for me to follow her. I smile as I do. The moment I'm in the office, I'll grab the gun. If I can sneak it back to Matt, we can figure out if it's loaded or not. The next opportunity we have, we'll use it.

We walk up the stairs and down the hallway. Instead of going to the office, though, she stops in front of the guest room.

"I want to write now," I tell her again.

She smiles at me. "I know you do. But I know what

you're hiding." My mouth drops. "You want to send an email out for help, don't you? Your publisher. Someone else, maybe. Anyone. All you have to do is tell them where you are." She lifts the knife to my face, putting it an inch away from my cheek. "No games, Sidney."

"I'm not trying to—"

"Stop!" Tess shouts. "I'm disconnecting the net. I'm moving the computer downstairs, where I can… watch you."

CHAPTER 43

Tess directs me inside the guest room and locks the door behind me. Matt sits up in the bed when I enter the room, a thin smile on his face.

"I was worried you wouldn't be coming back," he says. He takes a deep breath. "What did she say?"

I sit beside him. "She's crazy." I look at him. "She wants me to write her story." I shake my head. "According to her, she's killed many people. She actually said she wants me to make her famous. All of this was to get me here at this house so she could get me to do this. She wants me to write an entire book. She's planning on us being here for months."

Matt takes in my words. "What happens after the book is done?"

I shake my head. "We're not going to find out. As soon as I can get to that gun, we'll use it. She still doesn't know it's there. She thinks I'm trying to use my email to contact someone for help."

"You need to leave," Matt says.

I look at him and pretend he didn't say it. I walk to the door and try to open it. It's locked, of course. I heard Tess lock it before she left. I push my body against the door and feel it wobble.

"Do you think we can crack the door open?" I ask. "Can you manage to get here? We can use our weight and burst through."

Matt shakes his head. "She'll get upstairs before we can do anything… You need to leave."

I look around the room. "Maybe I can find a weapon. She has a knife. If I can find something, I just need to wait for an opportunity."

"You need to leave!" Matt shouts, immediately covering his mouth.

I look at him and hold my breath. "Matt, stop. We can—"

"No," he says softly. He points to the window. "You can get through that. I know it. Your scrawny butt finally has a purpose." He smiles at me.

"The drop is too high," I say. "I'll be as injured as you if I try."

Matt moves his body and shows the comforter that he's been weaving into a thick rope. "You use this to climb down as far as possible. It won't save you too much height, but you won't be dropping a huge distance. I'll try and lower you."

"Matt," I plead with him. "I can—"

He puts up a hand. "Sidney, stop. I can't get away." He laughs. "I won't fit through there. You can, though. When you do, use your plan to survive. Just like you told me: follow the gravel path to the main road. Find that small town." He looks outside. "Sun will be setting soon. Tess doesn't have a car. You can get some distance before she realizes you're gone. You just need a head start."

"Matt, I can't leave you."

He looks at me. "You already did leave me." He swallows hard.

I lower my head. "I'm not leaving you here to die."

He takes a deep breath. "I won't. She'll be distracted

when she finds out you're not here. Like you said, I need an opportunity and I'll get to the gun."

"You'll crawl to the gun?" I say, shaking my head. "That won't work."

He stands up from the bed and motions toward the window. He opens it quietly and looks at me. "It's time to leave. Get the bedsheets for me."

I look at him, his eyes watering. Tears of my own are forming. "We can work together," I say. "I don't have to leave you here."

"I want you to." He lowers his head. "One of us has to make it out of here. It needs to be you, Sidney. I know you won't say it back to me. I don't deserve it. I don't deserve you. Not after what I did." He takes another breath. "I love you, Sidney. I love you so much." Tears are now freely falling from his eyes. "I need you to make it. You need to escape. Please."

He lowers his head again. I walk past him and grab the rope he made from bedsheets and give him one end of it, tossing the other out the window.

I walk up to him and caress his face. "I do love you, Matt. I wish you knew how much I love you." I kiss him softly.

Matt looks at me and wipes my tears from my face. He grimaces in pain from his leg. "You have to go now, Sidney."

CHAPTER 44

With Matt's rope, I'm less than six feet off the ground when I drop. I stand up immediately, unharmed. Matt pulls in the blanket through the window. He stares down at me, and I look up at him.

Through the large windows on the ground floor, I see movement. I quickly duck as Tess walks across the room. I look up at Matt again, but he gestures for me to hide.

When I look inside again, Tess is staring out of the window next to mine towards the lake. For a moment, our eyes meet until I realize she's looking at her own reflection. She turns and walks towards the kitchen.

I let out a breath. When I look up at the guest bedroom window, Matt isn't there. Having nearly been caught by Tess, I know I need to leave. Matt's plan didn't involve me getting seen within the first few minutes of escaping. If he's to stay behind, he needs to ensure it's for a good reason. I quickly make my way around the house, being sure to stay low as I do. When I'm in the front, I see the long gravel road. There's a wide empty field I need to cross, though. There's a chance if I run through it, she'll see me. I decide to go around the longer way, through the bushes lining the path. It will add time to my escape, using up precious sunlight, but I don't want her to discover me.

Once I can barely see the lake house through the trees, I try my best to jog through the dense brush. A few times I nearly trip but manage to steady myself. I look back every so often, wondering what's happening with Matt. Was Tess planning on coming back into the guestroom soon? How will she react when she does?

Matt's strong but also vulnerable with his injury. He won't be very quick with his leg. He does outweigh Tess by quite a bit, though. Even if she attempted to cut him, there's a chance he'd manage to defend himself. He could overpower her.

I should have stayed. Why did I leave him? We could have taken Tess on together.

Soon I see a gravel road through the trees. When I step out onto it and look back, I can barely see the lake house. It's getting darker as well. I start sprinting down it, my mind thinking through everything that's happened.

Cole was murdered. Tess is a monster. I've left Matt alone to fend for himself with a possibly broken leg. The two innocent people in the basement cellar were killed.

Even if I escape and get to the authorities, what are the chances that Tess will still be at the lake house by the time I get back? She would leave. I'd forever be looking over my shoulder until she's caught.

How many more people will die because of Tess?

At least one more. Matt.

He told me to leave, I remind myself. I'm out of breath and slow my pace to a walk. I stop entirely and look back down the gravel road.

Matt's plan was for me to leave him to die. He wanted to ensure I escaped before he tried to get away himself.

When IWriteAlone entered my life, I became so

afraid. I barely left my home. I was scared to keep writing. I couldn't face my fear.

If I run now, my life will forever be as it's been for the past year. Worse. Matt may not make it. I take several deep breaths, thinking over my options. I look back at the path towards the house.

I'm not running anymore. I'm not leaving without Matt.

CHAPTER 45

As I get closer to the lake house, I see someone in the field outside. A flashlight is in their hand, and they turn it side to side frantically.

Could it be Matt? For a moment I desperately hope it is until I realize how easily the person is moving. Matt wouldn't be capable of that.

It's Tess.

Has she already discovered that I'm not in the room? I go through the bushes, the opposite way to where Tess is searching.

I quicken my pace and I worry what happened to Matt. I can only imagine Tess opening the door and not seeing me. She would have immediately closed and locked it. What if she didn't?

All I know now is that she's outside looking for me. But she's no longer inside the house. I just have to get to the office before her.

Tess flashes the light towards a tree in my direction. I freeze, thinking I'm caught, until the light moves away from me. Thankfully, Tess starts moving further away.

I go around the treeline until the front door is only a few yards away from me. I look from the door to Tess in the field. Her flashlight is still searching for any sign of me.

Now's my chance.

I bolt through the trees toward the house. When I get to the steps, I see the front door is partially open. I look back and Tess is still far off in the field and hasn't noticed me. When I quietly open the front door fully, an empty can drops from the top of the door frame, clinking on the floor loudly.

It takes me a moment to realize Tess placed it there. When I turn around, her flashlight is directly on me, and she's rushing towards me. My eyes widen as she gets closer. I slam the front door shut and lock it. I run up the stairs and nearly slip on the wet floors in the hallway.

I notice the guestroom door is shut and locked. I have no time to check in on Matt though.

I smile when I see the office. I quickly open the door and run to the desk. When I open the desk drawer panic sets in.

The gun is gone. She must have it. Or maybe Matt somehow got to it first.

I go back into the hallway and the smell of citrus hits me. I realize Tess has mopped the floor. My face drops, and I stand outside the guest bedroom door. I take a moment before I open it and step inside.

I cover my mouth immediately when I see him. Matt's sprawled out on the bed, not moving. Blood stains all the sheets red.

Tess storms up the stairs. I turn to meet her glare as she sees me. The knife is tucked into her jeans pocket, the tip of the blade sticking out. The gun is pointed at me.

CHAPTER 46

"I was about to give up looking for you," Tess says. "So happy you came back. Now we can finish the story."

"You killed him," I say. I can't look back at Matt. I can't see him that way.

"He tried to hurt me," Tess says. "He lost. He died trying to get to this." She turns the gun to the side and looks at it. "I didn't know about the gun. I see why you were so interested in writing tonight." She smiles. "Now I know I won't be able to trust you fully."

"You killed him," I say again.

"Stop it, Sidney," she says. "I did you a favor. You told me about the other woman. You found out what he did to you. I've done you a favor. If you want, you can include him in the book."

I look at her intensely. "You're insane... I'm not writing your book."

Tess points the gun at me. "Well, what use are you?" I stare at her. No matter what I do, my fate will be the same as Matt's. All of us will be in the wine cellar eventually.

Tess sighs. "Tomorrow, you'll get over this. It will be a new day. I'll tell you more about my story. Soon, you can share it with the world."

I'm not going to write a word.

I shake my head. "I don't care about your story." I

take a step towards her, but Tess moves back. I smile, realizing that she doesn't want to actually pull the trigger.

She needs me.

"Stop," she says. "I'll kill you."

"Do it," I say. "You're going to eventually anyway."

She grins. "Stop ruining the big twist of the book."

"That's not the twist," I say. She looks at me, confused. I smile back. "The gun isn't loaded." She brings it to her face to examine and as she does, I rush towards her, pushing her to the ground. The knife digs into her abdomen. She cries out, and I wrestle the gun out of her hand.

I stand up immediately and point it at her. While I've written many stories that use guns, I've never held one. What I do know is there's a safety. I see it and turn it off quickly. Instantly the power shifts between us as I point it at her.

Tess laughs as she slowly gets up from the floor, the knife now in her hand.

"It's over, Tess," I say.

She shakes her head. "No. It. Isn't!" She pounds her foot on the ground as she says each word. "This is not how it ends, Sidney!" She points the knife at me. "You really impress me. Maybe it's meant to be this way." She laughs. "The good guy is supposed to win at the end of a book, right? The villain gets the justice they deserve." She lowers her head, and stares at me. "It's the best way to end this." She takes a step forward and smiles at me. "Do it," she whispers.

I step back and aim the gun at her. "Just stop, Tess. This isn't a story."

"Do it!" she shouts, taking another step. She closes her eyes and grins. "Make me famous."

I shake my head. "Tess! Enough."

When I don't pull the trigger, she opens her eyes. Her smile leaves her face. Her eyes tense and stare at mine. She screams and begins to run towards me.

My finger pulls the trigger without me realizing. Tess shouts as the bullet rips through the center of her chest. She immediately collapses to the ground. Moments later, her blood begins to pool around her.

I look at the gun in my hand. It was loaded after all.

There's a phone in a box downstairs. I need to call the police, but I'm frozen by the sight of Tess. I almost expect her to come back to life like in the scary movies.

I turn and look back into the guest room. Matt isn't moving. He's gone. I take a deep breath, trying to figure out what to do next.

"Sidney," a faint voice calls out. "Sidney, help me." I turn, and Tess has turned over to her side and is staring at me. The fake Tess is looking at me now. The one that pretended to be timid and scared. The Tess Simmons I befriended. She reaches out her bloody hand towards me. "Please, Sidney."

EPILOGUE

Vanessa introduces me to the large crowd, who erupt with thunderous applause as I walk across the stage and stand at the microphone. I wait to speak, but the readers' claps and cheers only get louder.

I take in the moment.

When the noise begins to lessen, I clear my throat, and take a deep breath. "Epilogue. It took over an hour for the authorities to arrive at the lake house. By that time, Tess Simmons had expired from her wounds."

I take a deep breath, trying to get the image of her last moments out of my mind. "I sometimes wonder what my life would have been like had Matt and I gone back to Alberta instead of going to the lake house. Part of me knows I wouldn't have changed. I would still be scared. Scared of IWriteAlone. Scared of my readers. Scared to write again. Scared to let go of relationships in my life that weren't working.

"My past was in full control of my life and what I did.

"What happened at the lake house could have easily destroyed me. It should have. But when my darkest moments came, I stood tall. I found myself again... I wasn't afraid anymore."

I take a step back from the microphone as the crowd erupts even louder than before. Several people begin to stand up from their seats, followed by the entire crowd.

My new novel has been a huge hit. Within its first few days, it managed to outsell *My Life as a Killer* in its first week, and it's stayed high in the rankings since its release over six months ago.

The novel already has a huge following and has been optioned for a movie.

My publisher did something no one has ever tried before. A full reading of the entire novel. Guest speakers, celebrities, and authors read chapters. The publisher set up a special contest where one fan was given the opportunity to read a short chapter.

The epilogue, the shortest chapter in the book, was allocated for me. I was worried how it would go. Part of me thought I'd freeze on the spot, speaking to such a huge crowd. Given the terrible events that happened at that house, I wasn't sure if I'd be able to handle it. I'm beginning to surprise myself by how courageous I really am.

The continuous clapping and hollering of the crowd tell me I've done a spectacular job with my short chapter and my book.

Vanessa walks across the stage and hugs me tightly. "Great job, Sidney!" she tells me before going to the microphone.

"Thank you!" she shouts to the crowd. "Thank you for coming today. This was an epic reading of Sidney Meyers' novel. Nothing like this has ever been done before, but tonight was a huge success because of you, and of course, Sidney herself." She points to me. "Please, let's give Sidney another hand."

I nod and wave to the crowd as they clap again for me. When I was on stage, gazing out at the sea of my fans, I tried not to really look at anyone in particular. It was easier to present that way.

Now I'm starting to notice individual people at the event. Fans really went all out. One woman in the front row is smiling at me. I can't help but notice the black shirt she's wearing. On it in bold gold colors is the text, "Make Me Famous."

I take in a deep breath again. How macabre of the crowd to turn the last words of someone I killed into merchandise. I wonder, if I was to search on Etsy, if I'd see a few sellers with similar inventory.

When the crowd settles, Vanessa continues. "Sidney will be available for book signings for a limited time after the show. Please come by and visit her in the smaller hall that's attached to this room. We'll be opening doors in the next thirty minutes. Again, thank you for coming. This has been a full reading of Sidney Meyers' new book, *The Couple at the Lake House*."

I leave the stage with Vanessa as the audience continues to clap. She immediately ensures the signing area is set up for readers.

I sit at the table, stacks of my books beside me. A large banner behind me shows the cover of *The Couple at The Lake House* with an author picture of me.

Vanessa walks up, a cup of coffee in her hand. I thank her as she hands it to me.

"I'm sure this isn't easy, Sidney," she says to me. "Are you doing okay?"

I nod. "Perfectly fine." I've had plenty of therapy sessions since what happened. It took a lot for me to write this story about my life. I did it, though. I owed it to myself. I wasn't going to be afraid of my past any longer.

Vanessa gives me a thumbs up as she runs to leave. "By the way," I say to her. Vanessa turns to me. "I got your schedule for the book signings next month. No concerns with any of the dates."

Vanessa smiles. "Thanks, Sidney." She raises her eyebrows. "It's going to be a long few months for both of us, I think."

After a few minutes, Vanessa gets the staff to let in readers. One by one, I sign their books, speak to them, and take photos. One fan in particular catches my attention in the line. She has a wide smile on her face when it's her turn to approach me.

The woman with the "Make Me Famous" shirt smiles. "I'm your biggest fan," she says. She makes a face. "Sorry. That must be weird to hear, given what happened."

"Not at all," I say. After signing her copy, we talk for a few moments before she takes a selfie with me.

"I have to ask," she says with a thin smile, "did everything you wrote about actually happen?"

I nod. "It did, unfortunately." She thanks me again before leaving.

Vanessa had said it would be a limited signing. She did that on purpose in case I got worked up like I had in the past. I didn't. We went well past the original allotted time for book signings. I ensured I was able to speak to every fan who wanted to meet me. Take every photo and sign every book.

The publisher arranged for a hotel room connected to the convention hall. As I leave to head to my room, I continue to think about the events at the lake house. I think of the woman's question as well.

Did everything happen the way I wrote it?

For the most part it did.

However, I skipped over my last encounter with

Tess. I take a deep breath as I think of it. She called out to me for help. Tess crawled towards me, pleading. I could have done something. I'm not sure if I could have saved her from her wound. I didn't want to help her.

Ever since IWriteAlone entered my life, I've been afraid to confront my fears. What would my life be like knowing a woman like Tess Simmons was out there? Even if she was in prison, rotting for the quadruple homicide she committed at the lake house, I knew I would be forever worried. Scared that someday I'd see her again.

When you write a book, you want your main character to be somewhat likeable. Tess had told me that she was a storyteller. She manipulated people to see the story she wanted them to see. To see the good in her.

Well, I'm a storyteller as well. My story showed what I wanted, and left out the ugly truth.

As Tess pleaded for help, I aimed the gun at her head and fired.

Never again will I let something from my past haunt me in the future.

I'm not afraid anymore.

※ ※ ※

Note from the author:

I truly hope you enjoyed reading my story as much as I did creating it. As an indie author, what you think of my book is all I care about.

If you enjoyed my story, please take a moment to leave your review on the Amazon store. It would mean the world to me.

Thank you for reading, and I hope you join me next time.

Sincerely,
James

Download My Free Book

If you would like to receive a FREE copy of my psychological thriller, The Affair, please email me at jamescaineauthor@gmail.com.

Thanks again,
James

And now please enjoy a short excerpt from my book, *She Won't Leave*:

❊ ❊ ❊

SHE WON'T LEAVE

She has taken over my life.

Everything was perfect until tragedy brought my mother-in-law, Delores Sterling, to my front door with extra baggage at her side. After the sudden death of her husband, she asked if she could live with us temporarily.

I knew that living with my mother-in-law wouldn't be easy. She's made it obvious ever since I married her only son, that I'm not worthy of him. After all, I was his housemaid until he fell in love with the 'help', as Delores puts it. Because of that, I've kept her at arm's length, which was easy until she knocked at my door.

My husband doesn't see what she's doing to us. It's clear she has it in for me, and is destroying my marriage while living in my home.

But there's something even worse at play.

As Delores' presence at my home becomes more suffocating, I begin unraveling her dark secrets. The more I dig into my mother-in-law's past, the more I realize I'm fighting for more than just my marriage.

There's only room for one woman in my husband's life.

PROLOGUE

Delores

I was married for over forty-six years, until today.

Leonard and I may have had a long marriage, but none of it was the type of romance writers would describe. Our relationship didn't start with a bang, but it certainly ended with one.

I would like to say that we were happy together. In our defense, a few of the many years we shared were, possibly the ones where we were new to each other – but even those weren't amazing, to be honest.

Mediocre at best.

The powerful Leonard Sterling hated mediocrity, which seemed ironic when I think of our marriage. No matter how much money, land, or success he accumulated in his life, our marriage remained hollow.

I stare at a picture of us in our massive living room. The room shares dark features illuminated by the sunlight that pours through towering windows, casting a warm glow, highlighting the expensive furniture and drawing the eye to the large fireplace with its marble mantle.

We had everything in life anyone could ever want. A large, ridiculously expensive house. Maids, chefs, gardeners... People would believe that our life was as majestic as this beautiful home. No matter what expensive things we put in this house, this portrait of us never seemed to fit.

The picture of the "happy" couple, Leonard and Delores Sterling. We had a professional photographer take it for us a few years ago upon my request.

Leonard didn't care for it. He rushed me that day to get ready. He refused to go to the photographer's studio. He would only accept it being taken at our house or his office, where it was convenient for him to be available.

So we had the photographer take our photo of us in our home, in the living room. The same living room I stand in now.

Leonard sat in his favourite leather chair. I stood beside the chair, my hand on his shoulder. Even in pictures, we seemed so distant. No romantic embrace even for the small moments a camera lens can capture. We couldn't even pretend to be in love for the photographer.

Leonard demanded the photographer hurry and take the picture so he could return to his work. The man did as requested. One shot. That was all Leonard would allow. He gave me what I wanted. A picture of us hanging in our home. It's the only one of us in this house.

Instead of leaving to go to his precious office, Leonard took out a large cigar from his suit jacket. He lit it and sat in his favourite chair as the photographer dismantled his set-up.

We could have easily taken more pictures together. Maybe we could have pretended to be happy.

It never made sense why we couldn't have been. I was the perfect wife to my husband. I took care of my body, not letting age get the best of me. I threw myself at the man willingly, but he could care less, only willing to touch me on anniversaries or random nights for minutes of pleasure.

I was willing to be anything for my husband.

If a stranger was to walk inside my home and rummage around, they would have no clue who owned it, with this picture being the only evidence to support it was us. Leonard found it tacky to hang pictures of us on the wall, but I didn't care. Even he wouldn't stop me from putting pictures of my darling son, Leo, on the walls. I suppose the strangers who entered would assume that the small boy somehow owned this mansion.

We named Leo after his father, but my boy shares no characteristics of my husband. Caring, loving and always smiling, Leo is perfect.

Although my sweet boy's face reminds me of the love I still have in my life, he has grown much older now. He's become a businessman himself, much like his father. Unlike my husband, my son still attempts to have me involved in his life, even though it's less than I like.

Even when Leo realized what a wretched person his father was, my son still kept in contact with me, although it wasn't much. I was worried after their falling out that it would be the end of the only relationship in my life worth having.

Thankfully, that wasn't the case for a long time, until somewhat recently.

My son is married. He was naive, young and supposedly in love. In love enough to marry someone nearly as wretched as his father. He just doesn't see it that way.

His wife, Madelyn, may be sweet as pie, but she

doesn't have the background to deserve my son. She had nothing before my boy came into her life. She sank her claws into my son until he agreed to marry her.

Just like his father, she keeps me away from my son, but I won't allow her to do that any longer. My son has moved into a large house close to mine in Summer Hills. It's a small community in northwest Calgary where many of the wealthiest live. This should be an opportunity for us to see each other more, but I know she won't allow it.

He is my blood. She's the outsider.

It took me years to realize the mistake I made being with my husband. I hope I can help my son realize his error much sooner.

I pause a moment, staring at the picture of Leonard and me again.

I hung it in the same living room where the picture was originally taken. Part of me wanted it here to remind myself how infuriating it was being with a man like Leonard Sterling. To remind myself that he had all the power. He got what he always wanted.

I look over at my husband in the living room. He's still sitting in that chair. Instead of the expensive cigar being held tight in his mouth, it's dropped to the floor by his foot, embers still glowing. On the side table beside him is a rock glass with expensive scotch, his reading glasses, and a typewritten note left behind.

I light my own cigarette and enjoy the taste as I inhale.

Just as I did in the portrait, I stand behind my husband, placing my hand on his shoulder. I peer at the side of his head, where the bullet entered his skull. His body is slumped to one side, and his cold eyes are wide.

As I exhale, a plume of smoke covers my husband's

face.

As much power as Leonard Sterling had in his life, he couldn't control the silly expression his face made in death.

I need to call the authorities, but instead I stare at my deceased husband with amazement. He's dead, and yet it doesn't strike me the way it should.

Nothing about our relationship ever did. Forty-six years of marriage has come to an end, but I still have plenty of life to live.

CHAPTER 1

Madelyn

Please. Please.

I've only wanted one thing since I married my husband. Everything is perfect in my life. We've moved into what anyone would consider a mansion. Despite the stereotypes of wealthy men, my husband, Leo, is nothing that anyone would expect. He's caring and empathetic. He cares about my needs and the needs of others.

I knew he was different from the other rich people I've worked for.

Any woman would consider themselves lucky to be with a man like Leo. Not just because of his money, but he's a treasure of a human being. He's perfect.

I never thought my life would be easy. If anything, I figured I'd eke out a living cleaning homes for rich families my entire life. Scrubbing their expensive tiles. Sweeping their hardwood floors. Dusting their shelves with the expensive things they own on them.

Then I worked for Leo Sterling, and everything changed.

I look down at the test stripe on the bathroom counter. Waiting for the results kills me every month. I don't know why I do this to myself. It's almost a ritual of failure now. I think I enjoy tormenting myself with negative results.

I breathe in deep and think of where I started. I think of the first time I met Leo. He seemed so awkward giving me instructions on what he would like cleaned. Leo owned a much smaller house two years ago, despite it being larger than anything I would ever live in.

I remember how cute he appeared when gave me that wry smile while apologizing for telling me what he wanted me to clean. I tried to tell him that it was okay. I was used to it, after all. Usually, the instructions I received were much worse. Barely a hello from the wealthy homeowners I typically worked for. Those rich people would barely notice me in their presence, unless I missed a spot, then of course I'd hear from them.

Leo was different. He saw me. He spoke to me. He thanked me profusely after I finished. I have to admit, I took extra time to clean near his office to talk to him. He apologized when I entered and said he would move to get out of the way. I told him not to. I cleaned around him as he worked.

Not only did he greet me every time I came to his home, but he talked to me as well. It started off as small talk. I never got too personal with clients. My employer at the time warned us not to talk to the clients unless they approached you. I certainly never talked about my own life to customers, but Leo was curious.

How long had I been cleaning for? Did I have any siblings? Where are my parents from? I did my best to ignore that last question. My mother raised me on her own and she struggled financially all the time. My father passed away when I was young, and I never talk about him because of what he did. If I did, I'd worry people would have a poor impression of my family.

When I think back at our beginnings, I wonder if I told Leo sooner about my past if he would have even cared. I don't think he would have.

Over the course of a few weeks, we got to know each other well. By that time, he already knew more things about my personal life than my own friends.

It didn't happen quickly, but I soon felt tension around him. A good kind. The feelings I got in high school when a boy I liked would notice me.

It was getting harder to not say something. I didn't, though. I needed my job. I couldn't afford to lose it and the cleaning girl getting too flirty is a good way to get canned from the company I worked for. Besides, I wasn't the only maid he had. He had others come by during the week.

I wondered often about the type of conversations Leo had with the other girls who came to clean his home. One of them was my friend, Hannah. She was the entire reason why I got hired at the company to begin with, but I found myself getting jealous of her and the conversations Leo and her likely shared. She's a much prettier woman than me. I know that. Nobody would have to state the obvious.

Any man would love it if a blond bombshell like Hannah walked into their home with a duster.

I could easily imagine Leo Sterling being interested in a woman like Hannah. Who wouldn't be, after all? She had told me herself how nice Leo was. I knew that meant they talked. Despite our friendship, I didn't tell her what I felt for him. I didn't tell her how jealous I was that she got to clean his home on the days I couldn't.

But it didn't take long for me to see I didn't need to have those insecurities.

One day as I was cleaning Leo's kitchen, he walked up to me shyly. He asked me why I never asked about him. I was taken back at first, until he explained himself. He always asked questions about me, my life, my interests, but I never reciprocated.

He lowered his head and when he looked back at me, he asked me plainly. Was I not interested in getting to know him? He said he was very interested in me.

I apologized. I told him about the cleaning service rules.

Then, something magical happened. It was almost out of a romance comedy movie. He stared at me. He said nothing, and neither did I. His lips pursed as he looked at mine.

To hell with the cleaning service.

I slipped off my rubber cleaning gloves. He approached me and we kissed. The butterflies in my stomach wanted to explode out of me.

Things only became more perfect after. We began dating. Things got more serious.

And then he fired me.

No more cleaning his house. I was going to move into his home soon after. I felt like my life was a fairy tale. Cinderella found her Prince Charming.

As the saying goes. First comes love, then comes marriage, but...

I look down at the negative pregnancy test on the counter. I breathe out and pound the counter, tossing the strip in the garbage can.

Fairy tales have good endings though. I try my best to remind myself that every time I see the negative strip to not overreact. To not to get worked up.

Leo and I have been married for nearly two years now,

and it feels like I'll never be able to give him a child. I'll never have the family I dreamed of since I was a little girl.

I would joke with my mother when I was younger how I'd want five kids someday. She always laughed me off. I knew about my mother's troubles trying to get pregnant herself. I was a miracle child, she would say to me.

I walk out of the marble-floored bathroom and look at my new home. We only moved in a week ago.

The high ceilings above are adorned with antique molding and a large, dazzling chandelier that casts a soft, golden glow. In the center of the foyer stands a masterpiece – a spiral staircase, crafted from fine marble, which leads to an upper deck. Upstairs is even more breathtaking. Panoramic windows on one side face the nearby Rocky Mountains.

My kitchen has two large islands and space for a huge dining table. Currently it has Leo's older table from his last house as we wait for our new furniture to arrive. There are eight rooms on the main floor. The house itself is nearly ten thousand square feet.

We have a six-car garage. Of course, the first thing Leo did was renovate the garage to be more to his liking. He said what the owner had was dated. We've been parking our vehicles outside for now. Leo owns a black Escalade and a neon green Lamborghini. He's told me once we've settled in, he wants to take me car shopping as well.

Our home is beautiful, and I can't believe I get to live here.

I look at the barren walls. Some day, I want to fill them with pictures of children and happy family moments. I know I should consider myself lucky though.

If you were to combine the small houses down most

of my block growing up, it would maybe beat the square footage of my new home.

Leo doesn't get as upset as I do with every month that I'm without child. We have options, he tells me. If I can't get pregnant, we can use them. The people who say money can't solve their issues don't have any. Something I learned from being with Leo is that money most certainly does.

IVF is an option. I only want to use it if we have to, though. I want to do everything more naturally, but with every negative test, I'm starting to realize that may not happen. It's not that I look down on other pregnancy options. I may have to use IVF someday and I will be forever grateful that I live in a time where this exists to help me get the family I want. I can't help but feel like a failure, though.

Leo tries to tell me it's natural to feel that way. I can't help it. The failed test feels like it's ruined our day.

Today was such fun, too. Leo took the day off work to go furniture shopping with me. We have a lot more rooms to furnish and we conquered many of them today. He wanted to hire a designer to just get it done, but I wasn't for it. The one thing I loved working for wealthy families was seeing their decor. Taking in the beauty of the rooms and how they dressed them up.

Now I have my own mansion to do what I want with.

I have many ideas. I told Leo he didn't have to come with me if he didn't want to. Once he understood how much designing our home meant, he wanted to be there with me.

Like I said, Leo is different.

Maybe it was just my enthusiasm for decorating but he was just as happy as me today as we went to several furniture stores. He didn't even flinch when it came time to pay.

The numbers on the receipt would be enough to haunt me at night, but Leo paid it with one swipe of his credit card without a second thought. I hate to think of how many homes I'd have to clean to pay for just one of the pieces of furniture we ordered today.

Leo enters the front door looking serious, his cell phone held tightly to his ear. For a change he's not wearing a suit and tie but jeans and a shirt. He doesn't have to wear fancy clothes to look handsome.

"Hey," I whisper to him.

He gives me a thin smile. "Sorry," he says. "I know I said I wouldn't work today but Charles called. I had to take it. You understand, right?"

I nod reluctantly. Charles Rayer is my husband's business partner. Together they built Sterling and Rayer, a property asset company. Not a very unique name for a business, but together they manage a portfolio of properties in Calgary, Alberta and have big plans to expand their investments. I knew from the very beginning after getting to know Leo that I would not only be sharing my life with him but with Charles too.

If he's not with me, he's with him. Best friends turned business partners.

Leo walks past me into the empty living room, continuing to nod to whatever Charles is saying on the other end.

I want to tell Leo about the negative test. I just want his comfort in the moment. I need him to remind me that everything will be okay.

I get too worked up trying to get pregnant. I just want the perfect family to match my perfect life.

I had nothing growing up, and now I have the opportunity to give my future children everything I could never have. The idea of it brings a tear to my eye as I wait for Leo to get off the phone.

The stress is making things worse. My period was two days late. I thought maybe this time the outcome would be different. I told myself last month that I'd talk to my doctor about my fertility concerns if this month came and nothing happened.

I take another deep breath. Leo turns to look at me from down the hall and smiles at me a moment before continuing with his conversation.

Just that smile is enough to reassure me that everything will be okay.

I hear a curse and the sound of something rattling. Hannah walks down the large spiral staircase with two small boxes in her hand. She smiles and looks at me. I can already tell what she's thinking since I was in her shoes not too long ago.

Thank god I didn't break anything down the stairs or my employer would have got upset.

In this case, that won't happen since I'm her employer.

"Watch yourself," I say.

Hannah laughs. "I thought I was going down the rest of these stairs for sure."

"I nearly did that my second night here."

When Hannah gets to the bottom, I take the second box from her. We walk together into the kitchen. I open one of the boxes and start taking things out.

"You don't have to help," Hannah says. "I can do this."

"No way. I don't want to be one of those people," I joke. Hannah and I used to laugh about the rich people we worked for and how stuck up and snooty they could be at times.

Hannah opens a different box. "I'm just so happy that you gave me this job. Really, thanks. It was hard to get full time at the cleaning service."

I wave her off. "Of course. We need help, especially with unpacking. I just..."

"What?" Hannah asks.

"I don't want this—" I wave at the house, "—to come between us. I don't want our friendship to change. Promise me it won't."

Hannah lets out a sigh. "Well, if I don't promise that, will you fire me?" she says playfully.

I shake my head. "Not funny, and no, I won't."

The truth is I could never. I could find out Hannah had burglarized the safe in my husband's office and still not. She's been like a sister the years I worked for the cleaning service.

I was sad when we grew distant after I married Leo. I blamed myself for that. I should have done more to stay connected to her. When we moved here and Leo said we would need to hire a maid and gardener, I told him I knew who we needed.

Leo was concerned about hiring a friend though. I knew Hannah needed the money. Leo's paying her directly instead of a cleaning service too. That company gave us pennies off every dollar they made from their wealthy clients. Now Hannah gets all of that money herself.

She deserves it.

"If I ever become like one of our old clients, tell me," I say. "I mean it. It will be a nightmare for me if I ever do."

Hannah laughs. "Well, give me your nightmare any

time." She looks around the large room. "You didn't tell me how furniture shopping went."

I don't want to tell her everything. It's a stupid thought since she'll eventually see all the beautiful pieces herself, but telling her about it feels like showing off.

"It was great," I say, keeping my answer short on purpose. "The movers are bringing everything in next week."

Hannah takes out a large kitchen knife from a box when the loud ring of the kitchen phone startles me. I look at it a moment and Hannah puts down the knife in her hand. "I can get it," she says.

I wave her off. "No, that's okay. Thanks." I smile at her as I pick up the receiver. "Hello, Sterling residence." I cringe when I answer the phone. That was how I used to greet callers when I worked for others. This is my house, though. I need to get used to my own lifestyle now. "This is Madelyn."

"Is my son available?" the voice asks curtly.

She needs no introduction. The snooty tone which always has a hint of condescension, entitlement and dismissiveness, belongs to none other than my mother-in-law, Delores. As per her usual fashion, she doesn't acknowledge my existence. Not a hi to her daughter-in-law or any small talk whatsoever.

Just, put my son on the phone.

"Hey, Delores," I say, trying my best to be cheerful. "Leo is just on the phone. I'll tell him you called."

"That will not do," she says curtly. "I need to speak to my son now."

"Oh no, is everything okay?" I ask.

"My son," she repeats. I roll my eyes in response. Hannah looks at me, confused, but I nod to let her know

I'm okay.

I walk back into the foyer and see Leo pacing, still on the phone himself. "Hun," I call out to him. I step closer and get his attention. "It's your mom."

He looks at me for a moment. "I'll call her right back, okay?"

I nod and put the phone back to my ear. "I'm sorry, Delores, Leo isn't available."

I hear her scoff on the other end. "Tell my son his father is dead." She ends the call and the sound of the disconnected line beeps in my ear. I look up at my husband, and it must be apparent that things are not well, because his expression changes as well.

Printed in Great Britain
by Amazon